I0669836

Philip Phillips

Descriptive Guide to Philip Phillips' Illuminated Tours and

Illustrated Songs

Philip Phillips

Descriptive Guide to Philip Phillips' Illuminated Tours and Illustrated Songs

ISBN/EAN: 9783337194017

Printed in Europe, USA, Canada, Australia, Japan

Cover: Foto ©Andreas Hilbeck / pixelio.de

More available books at **www.hansebooks.com**

First * Night's * Program.

Synopsis of

PHILIP PHILLIPS'

Illustrative and Refined

ENTERTAINMENTS

Half Round the World,

FROM

New York over the American Continent to San Francisco,

THENCE TO THE

Sandwich Islands, New Zealand, Australian Colonies, Ceylon and Through India.

Tour of the world, beginning with

NEW YORK HARBOR. Fourteen square miles of land-locked water. Yonder the stately ships, the white-painted excursion boats, the swift-moving tug, the graceful yacht, the glancing blue waters lapping the foundation-stones of the greatest statue on earth—Liberty.

BROOKLYN SUSPENSION BRIDGE. Greatest bridge in the world! One mighty span 1595 ft. leaps the chasm between the piers which tower 277 ft. high. Total length 5989 feet, 85 ft. wide, 135 ft. above the water; unsurpassed panorama of the beautiful harbor.

BRIDGE AT NIGHT. Illuminated by the double rows of Electric lights, an archway of fire, a burning link between the two great cities. The reflection is seen for miles down the bay.

BROOKLYN PUBLIC SQUARE. The city of churches and long avenues, great municipal structures, and her towering church spires.

GREENWOOD CEMETERY. So picturesquely situated on Long Island's rugged hills! The magnificent city of the dead. Noted for its artistic and costly private mausoleums.

WALKING OVER THE BRIDGE. Take the broad foot-way in the center, 20 minutes of acreal walking. Cable cars rolling past on either side, 1000 ft. wagon ways outside these. This bridge cost 15 million dollars. You will never weary of gazing.

CITY HALL, N. Y. Composed of marble. Long, broad, low, ancient cupola—stands in the center of a six acre park of splendid shade, a fine breathing place, surrounded by towering business blocks and teeming streets.

BROADWAY. Travelers say there is none other like it! It bustles with life and a Babel of noises. Up from the Battery it throbs, pierced three miles away with the tapering marble spire of Grace Church.

CITY FIRE SCENE. The heavens aglow! The instant rumble of engines and rushing ladder companies, but protection is ample with 51 engines, 19 hook and ladder companies, and over 800 skilled firemen.

NIGHT SCENE. The flames leaping from windows and roofs. Triumph of the color artist. The awful and beautiful effect.

ELEVATED RAILWAY. A fateful and momentous question, "rapid transit" at last solved. Flying trains from the Battery to Harlem. Imposing night scenes, passing illuminations in mid-air.

CENTRAL PARK. Ah! that Paradise of Landscape! 843 acres, 2½ miles long. Elegant drive-ways, tempting by-ways, weird caves, scores of monuments, Egyptian obelisk. Ah! let that picture stay, and yet longer.

RUSTIC BRIDGE. See the graceful arch of the rustic bridge so faithfully reproduced in the water mirror. Entrancing vision of the beautiful lake, its crystal

waters lapping moss-covered rocks and banks. But stay! where do the substance and the shadow merge? 'Tis winter! and the merry skaters glide, collide and shout over its frozen surface until they fall.

WEST POINT ON HUDSON. In the midst of grandeur, our West Point, from whence come our Grants, and Shermans, and Sheridans! The home of the soldier in embryo.

HIGHLANDS ON HUDSON. Glorious Hudson, unsurpassed highlands, palisades and Sunny Side, Anthony's Nose, Sugar Loaf, North and South Beacon, where burned the signal fires of the Revolution, magnificent hills, with precipitous bluffs disappearing in the tortuous channel.

ALBANY. Quite ancient Albany, stretching away upon its sloping hills; high and conspicuous over all, rises giant like, the new marble Capitol, that is crumbling and old while yet new. Monument of jobbery and extravagance.

NIAGARA FALLS. Entrancing vision of earth and water. The awful plunge of the thunder of waters down 164 feet below, 18,000,000 cubic feet a minute. Exquisite rainbow effect. A final and farewell peep into the icy CRYSTAL GROTTO.

CANTILEVER BRIDGE. This great structure is seen as it spans across the raging, seething torrent. Marvelous engineering, a net-work of slender iron in mid-air. Done in Dec. 1883.

CHICAGO. By Michigan's fair waters, Chicago, risen from the swamps and from fire. Magnificent city, covering 35 square miles, push and prosperity, a second New York. Massive buildings, superior hotels, wonderful city.

ST. LOUIS. Mighty city of the West, by the Mississippi's broad, swift waters, palatial steamboats loading at her broad levee for the sunny south, and the farther west and north. But yonder, what triumph of engineering!

THE GREAT BRIDGE. The father of waters laughed at, and three mighty arches of steel gracefully curve from Missouri to Illinois. Finest specimen of the metal arch in the world, spans over 500 feet, double track railway beneath, 54 feet passenger and wagon way overhead. Capt. Eads' monument. Opened July 4th, 1874.

KANSAS CITY. A momentary glance to shape it in your memory, for remember, this is the Gate City to the great Southwest.

DENVER. With a glimpse into Larimar Street, a sample of the inexpressible march of progress and enterprise in the Great West.

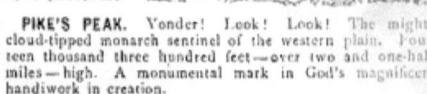

PIKE'S PEAK. Yonder! Look! Look! The mighty cloud-tipped monarch sentinel of the western plain. Fourteen thousand three hundred feet—over two and one-half miles—high. A monumental mark in God's magnificent handiwork in creation.

GRAND CANYONS, where scenes suggestive of the conflict of the gods thrill and awe the appalled eye.

NATIVE SUSPENSION BRIDGE swings yonder in rude picturesqueness, upheld by homely supports.

THE ROCKIES. The school-boy's dream! The tourist's ambition! How one gazes from the car-windows at their lofty outlines against the blue sky, and longs for exciting scalings of their granite walls.

STORM IN THE ROCKIES. Mighty and reposeful in peaceful sunshine, but how awful in the burst of storm-cloud and the rush of the rending winds and blasting thunderbolt. The skillful manipulations of

LIGHTNING EFFECTS enchances the awfulness and wierdness.

We approach the Gibraltar of the Mormon. Yonder is

SALT LAKE CITY, now clad in the fragrant garb of spring. Streams of pure water from the mountains flow along the side-walks, which are lined with numerous shade-trees, public squares and gardens, while high over all rises that domed temple of a peculiar faith, the

MORMON TABERNACLE, where an audience of eight thousand listened to the sweet songs of Israel as sung by Mr. Phillips.

A RAILROAD BRIDGE, with cars in motion, attests the skill of the genius at the lanterns.

NATIVE INDIANS. Repulsive but interesting and always picturesque is the native Indian squaw and papooses.

SNOW-SHEDS. Better looked upon than experienced! Those stern, hard necessities of a tour over the Union Pacific through the interminable snow-sheds; then we carve our way around

CAPE HORN, where scenes of the rarest beauty and sublimity meet the view—vast mountains, crystal rivers, sparkling water-falls, and lovely valleys until we reach Sacramento, capital of California (that state of golden realizations), picturesquely located on the Sacramento, fortified from the oft-raging torrent by formidable levees twenty to forty feet high. It has a $2,500,000 capitol building.

SAN FRANCISCO. Wonderful city, redeemed from shifting sand, city of the Golden Gate, the outlet to old ocean and the fabled East.

MARKET STREET, the Broadway of San Francisco, from the bay to the far hills; has many elegant buildings, and is a beautiful avenue.

MONTGOMERY STREET furnishes us with scenes of life and activity on every hand.

THE JOSS HOUSE. Quaint realization in Chinese architecture.

THE BAY OF SAN FRANCISCO. Beautiful! exquisite! a charm of nature's own choosing; the bay of all bays, and across it we glide bound for the Orient, with good-bye view of native shore, and a tear from glistening eyes as we pass through the Golden Gate.

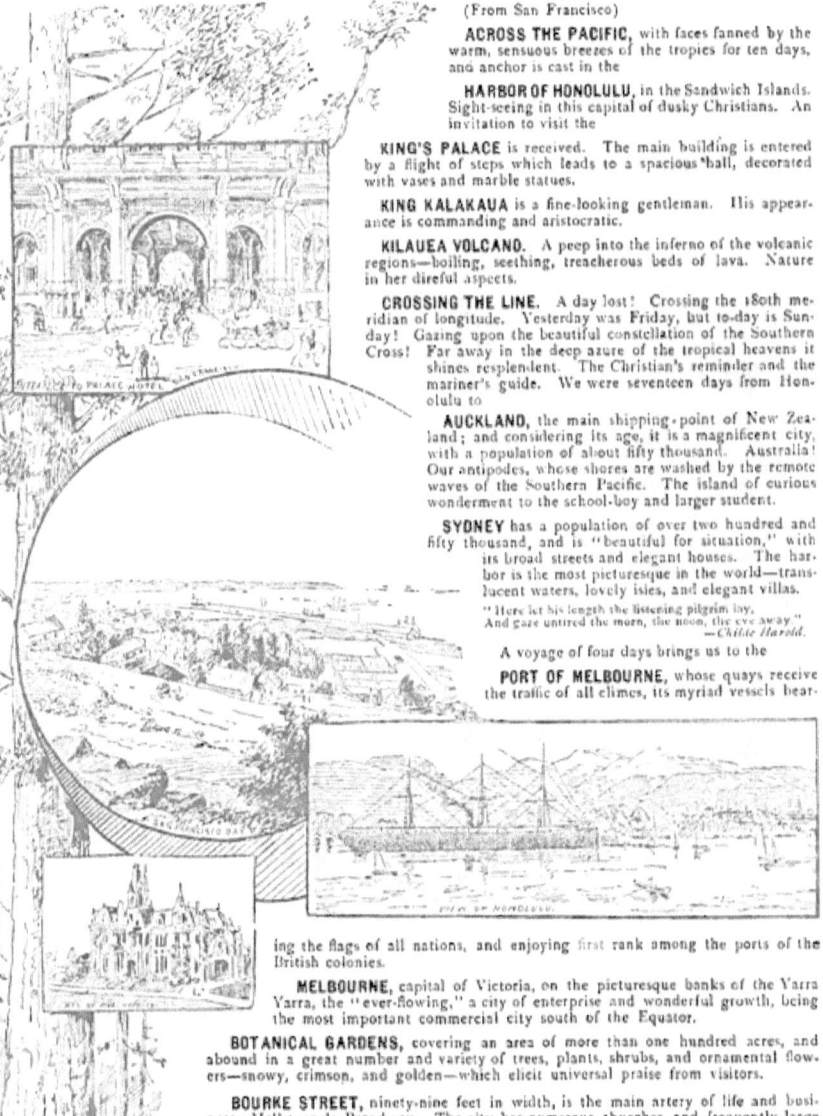

(From San Francisco)

ACROSS THE PACIFIC, with faces fanned by the warm, sensuous breezes of the tropics for ten days, and anchor is cast in the

HARBOR OF HONOLULU, in the Sandwich Islands. Sight-seeing in this capital of dusky Christians. An invitation to visit the

KING'S PALACE is received. The main building is entered by a flight of steps which leads to a spacious hall, decorated with vases and marble statues.

KING KALAKAUA is a fine-looking gentleman. His appearance is commanding and aristocratic.

KILAUEA VOLCANO. A peep into the inferno of the volcanic regions—boiling, seething, treacherous beds of lava. Nature in her direful aspects.

CROSSING THE LINE. A day lost! Crossing the 180th meridian of longitude. Yesterday was Friday, but to-day is Sunday! Gazing upon the beautiful constellation of the Southern Cross! Far away in the deep azure of the tropical heavens it shines resplendent. The Christian's reminder and the mariner's guide. We were seventeen days from Honolulu to

AUCKLAND, the main shipping-point of New Zealand; and considering its age, it is a magnificent city, with a population of about fifty thousand. Australia! Our antipodes, whose shores are washed by the remote waves of the Southern Pacific. The island of curious wonderment to the school-boy and larger student.

SYDNEY has a population of over two hundred and fifty thousand, and is "beautiful for situation," with its broad streets and elegant houses. The harbor is the most picturesque in the world—translucent waters, lovely isles, and elegant villas.

"Here let his length the listening pilgrim lay,
And gaze untired the morn, the noon, the eve away."
—*Childe Harold.*

A voyage of four days brings us to the

PORT OF MELBOURNE, whose quays receive the traffic of all climes, its myriad vessels bear-

ing the flags of all nations, and enjoying first rank among the ports of the British colonies.

MELBOURNE, capital of Victoria, on the picturesque banks of the Yarra Yarra, the "ever-flowing," a city of enterprise and wonderful growth, being the most important commercial city south of the Equator.

BOTANICAL GARDENS, covering an area of more than one hundred acres, and abound in a great number and variety of trees, plants, shrubs, and ornamental flowers—snowy, crimson, and golden—which elicit universal praise from visitors.

BOURKE STREET, ninety-nine feet in width, is the main artery of life and business—Melbourne's Broadway. The city has numerous churches, and frequently large assemblies gather in the parks for worship.

COLLINS STREET is one of the leading thoroughfares, and affords a proof of the wealth and enterprise of the city.

GOVERNOR GENERAL'S RESIDENCE is a most magnificent building, elaborately ornamented.

THE TOWN HALL seats four thousand people, and has an organ which cost forty thousand dollars.

BALLARAT. World-famous gold-fields. First nugget found here in 1857; views of mining districts; beautiful nature defaced by selfish man.

RAILROAD BRIDGE over the River Murray, which is low, muddy, and sluggish. Railroads are conducted after the English system.
Tasmania; wonders of

FERN-TREE GULLY. Ferns one hundred feet high, whose umbrella-shaped tops shut out the piercing sun-rays.

HUNTING KANGAROOS is a sport engaged in by both men and women. They go out on horses, and pursue their game at break-neck speed, riding over ditches and fences with impunity. An amateur hunter made sport of by these fleet leapers.

THROWING THE BOOMERANG. The untutored savage of the plain and his favorite projectile; a marvelous feat.

STEAMER EN ROUTE FOR CEYLON. From the deck of the out-going steamer we bid adieu to this continent island of the Southern Pacific, Australia! See the mechanical wave effects, and prepare for a twenty-two days' voyage. The many storms which we encounter make us realize the terrors of a storm at sea. Land ho! With the breath of spice-laden breezes in our nostrils our delighted eyes feed upon the palm-girt shores of Ceylon, and anchor is dropped off

POINT DE GALLE, where the cocoanut palm-trees wave their tufted fruit-tops among the cinnamon groves and coffee-bush. Instead of churches we now see heathen temples; instead of horses and carriages,

THE OX-CART, or "bandy," of the natives, a novel mode of Oriental travel.

CEYLON SEA-SHORE. Oh sweet realization of life-long dreams! Entrancing! Fascinating! One lingers in longing, gazing o'er pearly waters and scented shores, the spell only broken by the eager and importuning natives, who, with curious wares, swarm around you.
Wild, weird, in horrible grotesque, are the unaesthetic gyrations of the

DEVIL DANCERS. The natives believe that these dancers have medicinal power, and travel miles to witness them.

KANDY, capital of the dusky ancients of Ceylon. The scenery about this mountain-encircled town is magnificent and picturesque in the extreme.

CALCUTTA, city of palaces, approached by vessel upon the sacred Ganges, the panoramic view is a wealth of impression of Oriental opulence. Beautiful Calcutta!

THE GOVERNMENT HOUSE, as represented on the canvas, is very fine. Here is where the Viceroy of India resides. The botanical gardens are superior. Among its curiosities may be seen a

BANYAN TREE, the largest in the world, covering more than three acres of ground, its pendent limbs taking root and forming a forest of trees of lesser growth about the mighty parent trunk. A wonder in nature,

BENGALEE LADY in native dress, profuse in jewelry, quaint in arrangement, picturesque, a study for our American ladies.

AN ELEPHANT PROCESSION. Solemn, lugubrious, and majestic. These mighty quadrupeds bear aloft the idolatrous and superstitious natives in sacred pageant.
One of the memorable scenes in Eastern travel is the

HOOGLY, or Ganges River, filled with flitting crafts, which ply upon its waters of ancient superstition.

MAHARAJAH (Indian official), in magnificent costume of court dress, resplendent production of the oriental tailor. Gaze upon him and die.

o India was an occasion
e who saw it. On his
thundering of cannon,
the hearty acclamations

tropolis, holy city of the
the world, forever en-
ts of the generations of

rs naught but the living

ES is very repulsive, yet

ped form are the
efore these can be seen worshipers in solemn

A monkey god! Personification of the ridic-
of traditional devotion and loyalty to his
astime creature of the Zoo.
of former rebellion and mutiny, pictured in
f palaces and the elegant residences of the
nemory of history, and picturesque in pan-

ARDENS. While gazing upon the Memorial
eased eye feasts upon the wealth of Oriental
trained hand of culture.
MENT. The Angel of Peace guarding the
awful memory of massacre rises the carved
one. Ponder its lesson.

ow, will entertain the audience with some of the
nd effects ever produced upon the screen.

dest structure which
he memory of woman.
Shah Jehan for his
, "the Light of the

IGHT. We saw this
by the moon's silvery
rays it is a poem, a
s beneath the arched
d marbles, and gaze

atchless wealth of hu-
arble and inlaid with
flowers formed of pre-
d elaborately finished
composed of several

Great as are the di-
difices, it is as elabo-
tasket. That which
y to the Taj Mahal is
najesty and grace.
:yond the eye turns to

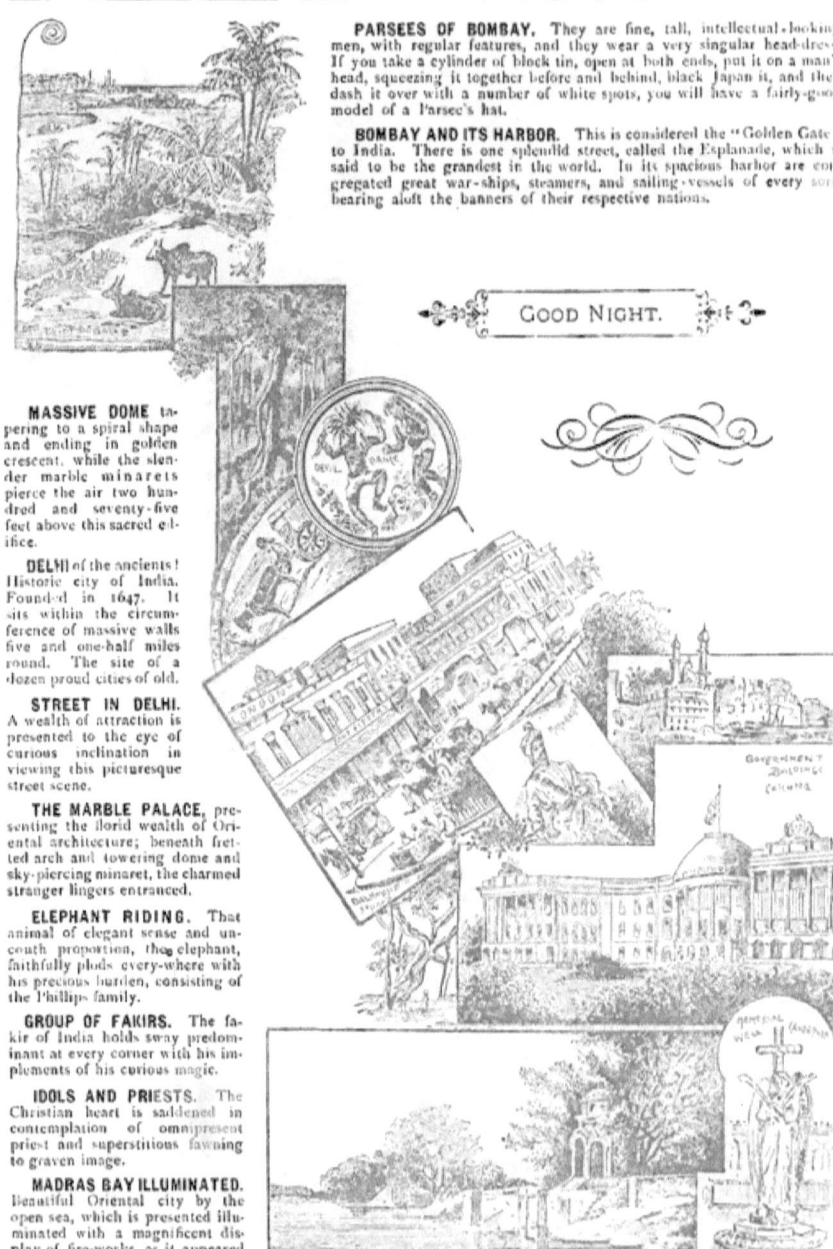

PARSEES OF BOMBAY. They are fine, tall, intellectual-looking men, with regular features, and they wear a very singular head-dress. If you take a cylinder of block tin, open at both ends, put it on a man's head, squeezing it together before and behind, black japan it, and then dash it over with a number of white spots, you will have a fairly-good model of a Parsee's hat.

BOMBAY AND ITS HARBOR. This is considered the "Golden Gate" to India. There is one splendid street, called the Esplanade, which is said to be the grandest in the world. In its spacious harbor are congregated great war-ships, steamers, and sailing-vessels of every sort, bearing aloft the banners of their respective nations.

GOOD NIGHT.

MASSIVE DOME tapering to a spiral shape and ending in golden crescent, while the slender marble minarets pierce the air two hundred and seventy-five feet above this sacred edifice.

DELHI of the ancients! Historic city of India. Founded in 1647. It sits within the circumference of massive walls five and one-half miles round. The site of a dozen proud cities of old.

STREET IN DELHI. A wealth of attraction is presented to the eye of curious inclination in viewing this picturesque street scene.

THE MARBLE PALACE, presenting the florid wealth of Oriental architecture; beneath fretted arch and towering dome and sky-piercing minaret, the charmed stranger lingers entranced.

ELEPHANT RIDING. That animal of elegant sense and uncouth proportion, the elephant, faithfully plods every-where with his precious burden, consisting of the Phillips family.

GROUP OF FAKIRS. The fakir of India holds sway predominant at every corner with his implements of his curious magic.

IDOLS AND PRIESTS. The Christian heart is saddened in contemplation of omnipresent priest and superstitious fawning to graven image.

MADRAS BAY ILLUMINATED. Beautiful Oriental city by the open sea, which is presented illuminated with a magnificent display of fire-works, as it appeared during the visit of the Prince of Wales.

SYNOPSIS

—of the—

SIGHTS AND SCENES

PRESENTED IN

PHILIP PHILLIPS'

SECOND EVENING'S PROGRAM

HALF ROUND THE WORLD,

—FROM—

Bombay through the Suez Canal to Palestine and Egypt,

ACROSS THE MEDITERRANEAN SEA INTO ITALY,

Over the Continent of Europe, England, Scotland and Ireland,

ACROSS THE ATLANTIC TO NEW YORK CITY.

Our second evening's programme commences with a bird's eye view of the

SUEZ CANAL. One of the world's great wonders of engineering triumph. The link of commerce between Old East and New West; one hundred miles in length.

BOATS PASSING UP THE CANAL. Compelled to run very slowly, and to go only by daylight, the sail is not a very enjoyable one.

Joy of the desert-worn traveler is the

OASIS IN THE DESERT, the fount of refreshing from the parching sand.

A glimpse of

PORT SAID, the Mediterranean gate of the famous canal.

Palestine! land of sacred memory. Our feet touch its soil at

JOPPA, and we gaze upon Christland from "the watch-tower of joy and beauty."

On to Jerusalem! A night's rest at the quaint old

RAMLEH, in an ancient and curious Latin convent. Jerusalem! From her memorable hills we gaze upon the city of departed greatness in silence and sadness.

THE JOPPA GATE. The traveler enters with strange emotions, longing yet fearing that this realization of Bible scenes made familiar must pain the Christian eye and heart.

In the city of sorrow, in the land of the prophets, we sit the first evening and look upon the

POOL OF HEZEKIAH with mingled emotions that drive sleep from weary eyelids; but our wakefulness is well repaid by one look at

HEZEKIAH'S POOL BY NIGHT. It is difficult to analyze one's feelings when looking upon such a scene as this, and to gaze upon

HEZEKIAH'S POOL BY MOONLIGHT, with the buildings illuminated and the soft moonlight reflected on the rippling waters, is more impressive still.

First morning in Jerusalem and in its early light, we view the

MOSQUE OF OMAR, site of Solomon's Temple. Beautiful structure! Its great dome kissed by the rays of the new rising sun.

MOSQUE OF OMAR ILLUMINATED. A faithful representation of the Mosque, as seen at night, with every window illuminated.

WALLS OF JERUSALEM. From the walls, battered by conquest and time's destroying march, one gazes from city to the valley of Jehoshaphat and Gethsemane's Garden, with the high peaks skirting the horizon.

GARDEN OF GETHSEMANE! Touched by the feet of the "Man of sorrows, acquainted with grief," "He who lived as never man lived, and spake as never man spake."

TOMBS OF THE KINGS. Amid the tombs of Israel's kings, whose memories for good or evil outlive the sealed sepulchres of decaying stone, one walks in the present and lives in the past.

JEWS' WAILING PLACE. The place of wailing. O scene of sorrow! With agonized forehead pressed to cold stone that is bathed in unsatisfying tear over fallen Jerusalem. Place of barrenness and grief unutterable.

CHURCH OF THE HOLY SEPULCHRE. Our picture gives a splendid view of this sacred edifice by night, and as we gaze upon it the windows are lit up, the moon comes out from beneath the clouds and sheds a brilliant light upon the scene. Under the open dome of the church of the Holy Sepulchre, the pilgrim gazes upon the

SEPULCHRE. In form of a miniature church, encased with profusely ornamented white stone.

INTERIOR. You enter, first the outer chamber, the "Chapel of the Angel," and bending low into the sepulchre where,

ILLUMINATED, forty lamps of gold and silver are kept constantly burning over the sacred tomb of Him! Oh! Him! Only in memory, for He is ascended, and the Infinite looks down compassionately upon finite man by these hollow walls circumscribed.

Out of Damascus gate, across the valley of Jehoshaphat, up the

MOUNT OF OLIVES, from whose heights the grand panorama of Judean hills spreads to the view, and all about is a sad reminder of grandeur and decay.

JERUSALEM IN HER GRANDEUR, giving a splendid panoramic effect, showing the city in her grandeur as seen in the time of Herod, with the triumphal entry of Christ into the city.

JERUSALEM IN HER DECAY as it appears to-day, with the Mosque of Omar marking the site of Solomon's Temple.

TOMB OF DAVID. By the tomb of David, "sweet singer of Israel," ancestor of Christ. Upon its rude wall the traveler bends the tear-dimmed gaze.

Straying in this land of holy memories, mid monuments and sepulchres of great and lowly, we pause by the

TOMB OF RACHEL, the lowly yet exalted. From here we go to the relics of ancient water supply, the

POOLS OF SOLOMON, excavated from the rocks, three in number, built with the science and method of requirement. The Gardens of Solomon were near by.

SHEPHERDS WATCHING THEIR FLOCKS. By night on Bethlehem's plain the shepherds watch their flocks, their thoughts attuned to the holy hush of night.

In holy awe upon their knees the watching shepherds fall, and the

ANGEL OF THE LORD appears and tells of "Peace on earth good will to men."

For in yonder depths of blue, overvaulting heavens, glows

THE STAR IN THE EAST, the beacon light of the world's salvation.

Most dear among the holy places of earth is

BETHLEHEM. Its houses of uncouth stone and vine-grown walls may lose form and substance, but the memory of the manger lives undimmed forever.

GROTTO OF THE NATIVITY. The alleged site of the Saviour's birth, where the silver star still keeps vigil. The sacred enchantment of the nearness of the spot to God's child's birth holds you in worshipful silence.

MARSABA CONVENT. Weird and dismal abode of the old monks, the wells and roof characterized by a fantastic display of human bones supposed to be those of departed monks.

THE DEAD SEA. Site of bitterness of once proud cities. At once inviting and repelling, it holds the curious traveler in transfixed gaze. Bathing experience often told.

THE JORDAN. "On Jordan's stormy banks I stand!" Aye, by its swift and muddy waters, aligned with willowy banks. Here the dove descended at the baptism, and here God's chosen crossed through the parted waters. Laving in the historic stream.

JERICHO. And the walls of Jericho fell at the trumpet's fateful blast to rise no more, miserable and decaying physical memento of the divine, avenging hand. Picture of desolation, of squalid hut and woe-begone, profligate native.

BEDOUIN THIEVES. Sons of treachery and deceit. Better viewed in picture than encountered in desert wilds. To see him is to "know" him.

BETHANY! Sweet Bethany! Home of Mary and Martha. Haven of rest for the God-Man in His weary pilgrimage on earth. Adieu, adieu, Palestine, thou land of prophet and fulfillment!

Land of the famed Nile, Egypt! Memory of the Pharaohs! In Alexandria's bay we cast anchor. Soon our eyes feast upon scene and house of European and Oriental beauty in the

GRAND SQUARE ALEXANDRIA. Thrilling sight of England's proud monsters of the waves.

BOMBARDING THE CITY. Devastation hurls down its fiery blast, and we now behold the square

IN RUINS. The devouring flame and smoke is seen arising. Graphic and fateful scenes.

PANORAMIC VIEW OF CAIRO. City of much beauty, tinged with the picturesqueness of age and decay.

TOMB of ABRAHAM PASHA. Beneath this famed golden and handsome tomb rest the remains of Abraham Pasha.

THE KHEDIVE'S PALACE. A maze of royal realization in architecture, with its grand corridor of myriad pillars.

MARBLE WALKS. Its stretches of marbled walks mid vistas of tropical shrub and flower. Reflection of evergreen trees in the mirror bosom of yonder

IMPRISONED LAKE, a place to wander and dream over the days of Joseph and the mighty Pharaohs. Who has not read and dreamed of

THE NILE, river of everlasting mystery. The artery of life to Egypt's narrow bounds. Again, those magnets of the traveler's gaze — the pyramids — rise from out the Egyptian sands to over-arching blue. Wonders!

PYRAMIDS AND UNDERGROUND PALACE. This picture gives the best idea of these immense stones polished in the highest style of art. How they were brought to this spot remains a mystery to this day.

Our privileged gaze is now fastened upon that wonder of human accomplishment crouching in the shifting sands,

THE SPHINX. Its stony, far-off gaze belongs to the past of thousands of years.

A lingering look across

ALEXANDRIA'S NOBLE BAY, whose waters lave the shores where Pompey's Pillar points to the vaulting blue, and old Egypt is bade adieu.

MESSINA. Come, fellow-traveler, we cross the blue Mediterranean, the tideless inland ocean, and anon our enraptured sight rests on Italy's sunny shores in the Isle of Sicily, off Messina.

MOUNT ÆTNA. Yonder Mount Ætna's famed peak towers with filmy smoke, ever ascending as from a mighty censer of nature.

NAPLES AND BAY. "See Naples and die." Often repeated like the old, old story, and yet ever new to the charmed traveler. Look! upon yonder dreamy bay, with its quaint crafts, then view palace and villa, and the half amphitheater sweep of the wharfed shore. Oh! theme of the poet's inspiration and minstrel's song!

NAPLES BY NIGHT. Entrancing by day, enrapturing by night. Lights of the city and gleam of fiery Vesuvius reflected in the vast stretch of limpid waters.

MOUNT VESUVIUS IN ERUPTION. Mount Vesuvius in angry mood of nature. Vivid flame of molten lava outpouring, and heaven-obscuring smoke. Such is this tyrant in active eruption.

In the

BLUE GROTTO, CAPRI. Lovely isle! The faithful camera makes possible your pleasure of to-night's glimpse of its wonders and peculiar beauty.

POMPEII. City of ashes, partly exhumed to the latter-day gaze of earth's wondering wanderer. One-half still is sepulchered. You wander amazed by long reaches of solidly-built stone-houses, perfect in pillar and post, but roofless. Upon temples, halls, baths, bake-shops, theaters, and mosaics of unimpaired luster you peer with eye astonished.

LAST NIGHT IN POMPEII. The last night of proud greatness may be thus idealized in the view we see, the refugees overtaken with the scoria and ashes.

Mecca of the tourist,

ROME, the city of seven hills, where Cæsar's name stood before all the world. From the dome of mighty St. Peters we look upon the once mistress of all the world, still mighty in her weakness.

THE COLOSSEUM. Picturesque and mighty relic of the once famed temple dedicated to murder and cruel sport for the edification of savage royalty and plebeian. Listen! These crumbling stones still are echoing the dying wail of human sacrifice and martyrdom.

COLOSSEUM—INTERIOR. Depicting a painfully dramatic and thrilling scene of the Christian martyrs thrown to the wild beasts,

COLOSSEUM; INTERIOR; NIGHT. Night falls upon the scene, and the beautiful angels descend and are seen hovering over the prostrate forms to comfort the dying, or bear aloft the spirits of the dead.

THE VATICAN, giving a charming view of the Pope's library, where may be seen some of the most beautiful and costly books ever printed. In the Vatican we view the masterpieces of the master-artists of all time:

RAPHAEL'S "MADONNA" and the

LAST COMMUNION, are renowned the world over as remarkable gems.

ST. PETERS AND CASTLE OF ST. ANGELO. A magnificent day view, with the river Tiber in the foreground, the sun gradually fades in the west, and our eyes rest upon

ST. PETERS AND CASTLE OF ST. ANGELO BY NIGHT, with the dome of St. Peters illuminated, and a fine display of fire-works from the Castle of St. Angelo.

ST. PETERS—NEAR VIEW. The greatest church in the world. Michael Angelo's triumph of hanging the Pantheon in mid-air bears realization here. We gaze upon the imperious facades and heaven-topping dome.

ST. PETERS—NIGHT. Night view of this handsome specimen of perfection in church building. Indeed the most glorious structure that has ever been applied to the use of religion.

ST. PETERS ILLUMINATED. As seen during a service on Christmas night. Three and a half centuries passed from its foundation (in 1450) till its completion as you see it to-night.

ST. PETERS—INTERIOR. Perfection of finish and adornment. Altars of purest marble, pictures of exquisite mosaics, walls of emblazoned gold, gorgeous frescoes. Wonder! Ponder! In dumb amaze you look upward into the vaulted span of that mighty dome as into the sky. So great in height that the floods of Niagara could pour therein in ample room.

ST. PAULS—INTERIOR. Modern built edifice of a progressive church. Its twelve pillars said to have been brought from Solomon's temple.

FLORENCE. Beautiful city of the flowery plain. Home of refinement and art. The famous church Santa Maria Noriello, "the bride" of that great artist, Michael Angelo. No one goes to Florence without visiting the celebrated

UFFIZI GALLERIES, containing the richest collection of paintings and statuary of earth. Here is the "Venus de Medici." Inspiration of pencil, brush, and chisel.

MILAN CATHEDRAL. The crowning triumph of Michael Angelo. Built of purest white marble, its spires and statues and carvings forming a fretwork of angelic beauty against the Italian sky.
Massive yet delicate to exquisite nicety in finished detail.

MILAN CATHEDRAL AT NIGHT. Indescribable by day—a dream of loveliness by night! Etherealized by the refulgent rays of the soft beaming moon.

VENICE. City of the sea. Queen of the Adriatic. Palace of the Doges. Streets of water. Wondrous city, the marvel of the tourist.

VENICE BY NIGHT. Enchanting scene! Dream of the poet! Inspired theme of master pens! Peerless Venice!

GONDOLAS. Swift-flying gondolas, with graceful prow, deftly propelled by ye gondolier of song and story. Gracefully he stands in poise, alert, guiding his peculiar craft with fearless and practised dexterity through winding canals.

ANCIENT SCENE IN VENICE. A night of memory in fair Venice. A scene on the Grand Canal by moonlight. Guests arriving in gondolas are passing up the brilliantly illuminated stairway of the magnificent palace, forming a characteristic view of Venice.

> By way of variety the Artist, Prof. Morrow, will here introduce some special mechanical effects of picturesque beauty and astonishing ingenuity. Richly-colored scenes, wonderful transformations, and illustrated records or songs.

PALACE OF BERLIN, home of the Kaisers, royal structure of the Hohenzollerns Unter den Linden.

THE ALPS, the incomparable Alps and the sage of mountains, Mont Blanc, with a view of "Arrowy Rhone," swift-flowing river in its ice-fed waters rushing from the boundless Alps.

PARIS BY NIGHT. Paris the beautiful, the dream of fair women, the ideal of adoring man! Gay Paris; pleasure, splendor and pageantry in endless panorama; civilization's kaleidoscope by day and night.

PARIS ILLUMINATED. Mirth, fashion, revelry on every side under the gas light; gay, giddy, godless Paris.

View of the

CENTRAL PAVILION of the famous exposition of 1867; scene of the last peaceful assembling of the crowned heads of Europe.

PLACE DE LA CONCORDE. Beautiful to the eye of the latter-day tourist, but of fateful memory of the bloody guillotine of the Reign of Terror.

VERSAILLES' GARDENS. Glimpse of the wondrous gardens about the famed Palace of Versailles, with realistic view of the sparkling fountains of that retreat of French royalty and later Republic.

HOTEL DE VILLE. City hall redeemed from the flames of anarchy, it stands the peerless official palace of the fair municipality.

HOTEL DE VILLE BY MOONLIGHT. Viewed in the soft radiance of flooding moonlight, its elaborate facade of graceful pillar and carven statues and ornate detail is well worthy a tablet in the page of memory. To

AMSTERDAM in old Holland, the metropolis city of pleasing and picturesque architecture; snatched from the embrace of the sea by the unconquerable and uncompromising Dutch. Ribboned by canals and laced together by hundreds of bridges; rare old city.

ROTTERDAM—lesser mate to Amsterdam—a city of commerce and opulence, ever wearing the good old Dutch flavor.

LONDON—London, mightiest city of earth; people of our tongue; mother city of mother England; yonder St. Pauls mighty, high-lifting dome; here the Thames and old London Bridge, Westminster Abbey, the Parliament Houses. Oh! city of tradition, of history, of chivalry, of royalty! One of the very first objects sought is

THE TOWER OF LONDON. From William the Conqueror to now the warp and woof of its history is woven in blood-red threads, dyed in the outflowing life-currents of the ill-fated beings who fell under the ban of royal whim and displeasure.

THE TOWER IN FLAMES. Once the stronghold and fortress of savage conqueror, we now see it in flames. But though destroyed several times, it has been rebuilt, and is now the museum of rude implements of war and famous

CROWN JEWELS. These are the jeweled crowns of England's kings and queens down to Victoria. $20,000,000 are here represented in crown and scepter and royal jewel.
Down by the

THAMES EMBANKMENT. There the Thames blackened by the hulls of the world's commerce. Here the swift penny ferry, darting up and down the busy river, the thronged bridges, while far up and down sweeps the giant stretch, world-renowned public improvement, the Thames Embankment.
View of

WATERLOO BRIDGE, built in commemoration of the victory of Wellington over the mighty Napoleon.
Who has not read of

THE CRYSTAL PALACE? From the beautiful stretch of magnificent park it rises a mighty palace of blue-painted iron and glass two thousand feet long. Massive yet delicate, majestic in nave and trancept, yet graceful in sweeping curves.

CRYSTAL PALACE—INTERIOR. Marvelous without, entrancing within. It seems incredible that a building so light-appearing and lofty

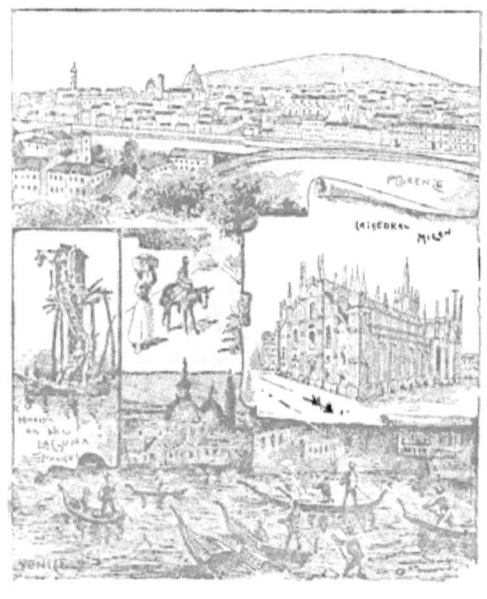

could overtop so vast a reach of space; an audience of fifty thousand listens to a service of song.

TRAFALGAR SQUARE—surrounded by stately residences, and from its center rises the lofty monument to Lord Nelson, the hero of Trafalgar.

WILD SCOTCHMAN TRAIN. The road beds of the railways of England and Scotland are of such perfection of construction that such express trains as "The Wild Scotchman" will run at the rate of sixty miles an hour between London and Scotch cities.

RAILWAY ARCHES. Railways in England are always carried above or beneath a crossing, thus many beautiful railway arches are greeted by the traveler's eye.

EDINBURGH, capital of the uncompromising Scot. Princess street, combining the ancient and modern in crumbling palace, magnificent monuments and later buildings of residence and commerce; a rare old street.

In Scott's "Heart of Mid-Lothian" is given an ever-to-be-remembered description of

EDINBURGH FROM THE CASTLE, a magnificent sweep of towering highlands; Holyrood Castle, crumbling and hoary, memory of Mary Queen of Scots. No view of Europe more fills the admiring eye.

ABBOTSFORD, the elegant residence of Sir Walter Scott, built on the banks of the Tweed,

amid a profusion of lilac, laburnum, and shrubbery.

BURNS AND HIGHLAND MARY. Always with scenes and thoughts of the Land o' Cakes comes the memory of Burns and his Highland Mary.

BALMORAL CASTLE—Queen Victoria's royal home in the Scottish highlands. From the portals of the stately castle the hills sweep away in unsurpassed magnificence and inspiring beauty.

BALMORAL CASTLE ILLUMINATED—as seen at night during a grand reception or ball.

VICTORIA, queen of England's mighty people, crowned in her childhood, in 1837, at seventeen, honored and revered in her fullness of years of beneficent rule.

GLASGOW, city of manufacture and of the famous Clyde-built vessels. St. Georges Square is always sought by tourists. It is grand and famous.

BOATS ON THE CLYDE. The most famous ship-yards of modern times are those of the Clyde. One of the most entrancing sights is a view of the Clyde and its myriad craft stemming the sparkling waters.

In old Ireland, land of incomparable beauty and song.

BELFAST, capital city of the North; thrifty, clean, and progressive. Our view is taken in

HIGH ST., showing the Albert Clock tower.

DUBLIN — SACKVILLE STREET is one of the great thoroughfares and fashionable promenades of Ireland's metropolis, and undoubtedly one of the finest streets in Europe; thronged with Irish jaunting cars and with the noble pillar of Lord Nelson in the center,

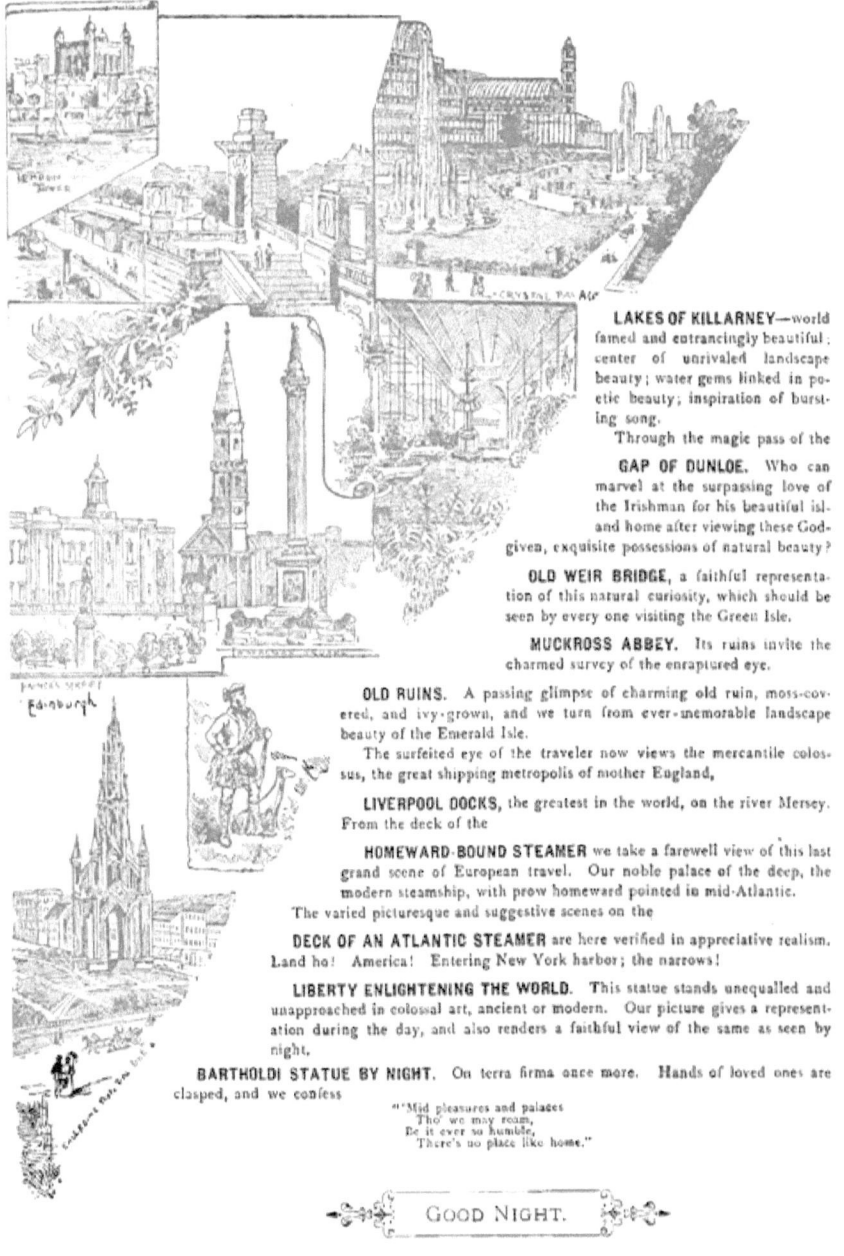

LAKES OF KILLARNEY—world famed and entrancingly beautiful; center of unrivaled landscape beauty; water gems linked in poetic beauty; inspiration of bursting song.

Through the magic pass of the

GAP OF DUNLOE. Who can marvel at the surpassing love of the Irishman for his beautiful island home after viewing these God-given, exquisite possessions of natural beauty?

OLD WEIR BRIDGE, a faithful representation of this natural curiosity, which should be seen by every one visiting the Green Isle.

MUCKROSS ABBEY. Its ruins invite the charmed survey of the enraptured eye.

OLD RUINS. A passing glimpse of charming old ruin, moss-covered, and ivy-grown, and we turn from ever-memorable landscape beauty of the Emerald Isle.

The surfeited eye of the traveler now views the mercantile colossus, the great shipping metropolis of mother England,

LIVERPOOL DOCKS, the greatest in the world, on the river Mersey. From the deck of the

HOMEWARD-BOUND STEAMER we take a farewell view of this last grand scene of European travel. Our noble palace of the deep, the modern steamship, with prow homeward pointed in mid-Atlantic.

The varied picturesque and suggestive scenes on the

DECK OF AN ATLANTIC STEAMER are here verified in appreciative realism. Land ho! America! Entering New York harbor; the narrows!

LIBERTY ENLIGHTENING THE WORLD. This statue stands unequalled and unapproached in colossal art, ancient or modern. Our picture gives a representation during the day, and also renders a faithful view of the same as seen by night.

BARTHOLDI STATUE BY NIGHT. On terra firma once more. Hands of loved ones are clasped, and we confess

> "'Mid pleasures and palaces
> Tho' we may roam,
> Be it ever so humble,
> There's no place like home."

GOOD NIGHT.

THIRD EVENING'S PROGRAM.

~SYNOPSIS~

— OF THE —

GRANDEUR AND GREATNESS

— OF —

PICTURESQUE AMERICA

AND

BRITISH COLUMBIA,

INCLUDING THEIR

Biggest Things from Ocean to Ocean,

AS EXHIBITED IN

PHILIP PHILLIPS'

ARTISTIC AND PATRIOTIC

ENTERTAINMENT.

Our third evening's entertainment will begin with a

MAP OF AMERICA. The magnificent sweep of God's country, the United States, from blue Atlantic to broad Pacific, and from the lakes to the Gulf. Land of the free and home of the brave.

WASHINGTON'S DREAM. The dream of Washington, mid the snows and bitterness of Valley Forge, of an incomparable empire of freedom and progression, glorious realization of to-day.

WASHINGTON'S MONUMENT—Cloud piercing; by the borders of the Potomac's fair waters; highest monument in the world; memorial stones contributed from the borders of the earth; its ambitious height is five hundred and fifty-five feet; begun in 1848.

THE NATIONAL CAPITOL, most stately temple of justice and law-making, costing $15,000,000; seven hundred and fifty feet in length; to top of the dome, topping statue of Liberty, three hundred seven and one-half feet; House and Senate wings of pure white marble; present edifice commenced in 1821.

NATIONAL CAPITOL ILLUMINATED—As seen during a night session.

THE PATENT OFFICE—Built in the Doric style of white marble and sandstone.

INTERIOR PATENT OFFICE, with vast collection of crystallized ideas of inventive brains stored here; interesting, fascinating.

TREASURY DEPARTMENT, palace of glistening and clinking coin; in the Ionic style of architecture, five hundred and eighty feet long, three hundred wide; stately column, thirty-one feet high, in grand perspective.

THE WHITE HOUSE, home of the presidents; its broad facade gleams white and cool through the vistas of fine trees; an enchanting spot.

WHITE HOUSE—EAST ROOM. The famous East Room, spacious chamber of stately levee; portraits of the presidents on the walls, massive and glittering chandelier, finest Turkish carpet, gorgeous upholstery of red; a sumptuous apartment.

WASHINGTON, Father of our country, the hero of a mighty nation enshrined in the hearts of her people.
Upon the martyred

LINCOLN, he who guided the ship of state with unfaltering courage and wisdom in her dark hours, we bend our honoring gaze.

GRANT, the great captain, the indomitable defender, he of Appomattox, who now sleeps by the beautiful waters of the Hudson. His memory will ever be honored till the reveille of the final awakening.

THE WAR, STATE, AND NAVY DEPARTMENTS—Splendid pile of Italian renaissance, built of granite, begun in 1871.

SMITHSONIAN INSTITUTION—Treasure house of na-

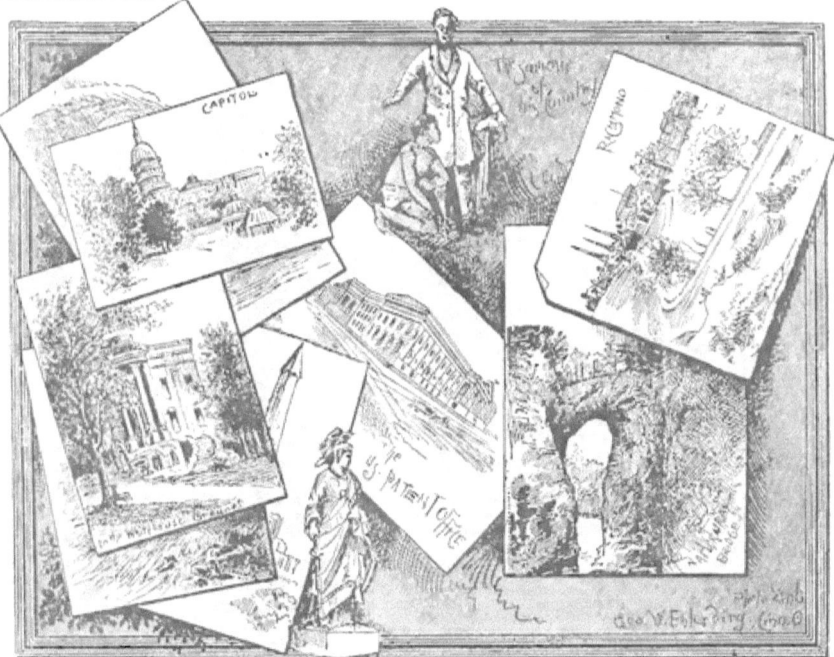

tional curios, a picturesque building of red sandstone, in the Norman Gothic style.

A charming view of

THE POTOMAC'S broad and peaceful waters, girt by the picturesque shores of "Maryland, my Maryland" and old Virginia, "all quiet."

RICHMOND, capital of Virginia and typical Southern city, picturesquely located upon a group of hills, and looking down upon the James River.

The most conspicuous edifice in all the city is

THE CAPITOL, designed by Thomas Jefferson. In the esplanade stands a remarkable statue of Washington, surrounded by other celebrated sons of Virginia.

WASHINGTON'S HEADQUARTERS. The old Revolutionary headquarters. Scenes of the battle plannings of our colonial days are still seen and much visited.

NATURAL BRIDGE. Wonderful product of nature's architecture. Higher than Niagara's towering fall, it rises in sheer precipice of granite wall with rock firm, buttress high, o'erspanning where the myriad names of ambitious climbers are cut in homely tablet.

FORT SUMTER. In peace its crumbling walls rise from out the waters of Charleston's harbor, a monument of rebellion's fateful downfall.

FORT SUMTER IN FLAMES—As seen after the bombardment, with the stars and stripes still floating proudly to the breeze.

CHARLESTON EARTHQUAKE. A view of Charleston, South Carolina, city of the nation's concern when dread earthquake crumbled her fair walls. Its awful effects still discernible in patched wall and redeemed edifice.

Realistic picture of a

SOUTHERN SWAMP. Weird scene of deathly quiet, drooping limb and decaying trunk, moss-covered and rank overgrown, lurking crocodile and noisome reptile; a scene of fascinating repulsiveness.

FLORIDA. Land floating in perfumes. Perennial delight of orange grove and pine-apple and waving palm; Mecca of the winter tourist.

COTTON PICKING. What more quaintly picturesque scene could be imagined than this one in black and white—darkies picking the snowy cotton crop.

A PLANTER'S HOME in Louisiana in the good old days befo' de wah! Realization of ideal comfort in ample rooms, broad balconies, and antique gables.

NEW ORLEANS—City ever fragrant with the bloom of magnolia and orange-blossom and foreign air of continental city; blending of the antique and modern in house and folk; our greatest cotton port; enjoyable city.

A ride through the leading thoroughfare,

CANAL STREET—Pleasant houses, with green blinds and vine-laden verandas, cool portico, and quaint colonnade; ideal Southern street.

MIRROR LAKE

Wonders of heaven-reaching grandeur in wood,

BIG TREES OF CALIFORNIA, the ever-awing sight and theme of never-tiring tale of the tourist.

YOSEMITE VALLEY, nearly six miles in length; nature's garden-spot of the world; grandeur and delicacy, exquisite bloom of myriad flowers, o'erleaping cascade, mighty tree, bold bluff, paradise of the gods!

From the brow of yonder bluff the watery sheen of the

BRIDAL VEIL FALLS, leaps and spreads its nine hundred feet of silvery and misty folds over the face of the giant rocks.

EL CAPITAN ROCK. Stupendous block of granite projecting squarely out into the valley with a vertical sharp precipitate edge three thousand three hundred feet high; seen for sixty miles.

Gazing into the clear bosom of

MIRROR LAKE, whose crystal waters reveal the secrets of its transparent depths, and reflect the beauties of nature; rare indeed.

Sacramento City, capital of California, possesses a beautiful

CAPITOL BUILDING, situated in a beautiful park covering eighteen blocks.

OAKLAND, the Brooklyn of the Pacific coast, and view of its great stretch of railroad piers.

TEXAS, "The Lone Star State" of superabundant plain and aristocracy of

CATTLE RAISING. Graphic view of cow-boys and their herded quadruped wards. Through

NEW MEXICO. Homely hamlets of

ADOBE, or sun-dried brick, more picturesque than comfort-giving.

A STRAW COTTAGE and its inhabitants, conundrum as to which is the homelier.

In California, tropic-touched clime

LOS ANGELES, metropolis of Southern California; orange-growing center; its streets ever cool in inviting and shaded walks; sought of the invalid longing for balmier breathings.

SAN FRANCISCO, with a population of three hundred and fifty thousand made up of all nations.

THE NEW CITY HALL is one of the finest municipal buildings in the United States.

THE U. S. MINT is a massive stone structure in the Doric-Ionic style.

MT. SHASTA, grand, lofty, magnificent sentinel of mighty nature; cold, lonely, and snow-capped; so well described in Joaquin Miller's lines, "Lone as God."

COLE'S STATION. In this enchanting land you find the model stage-driver, with his splendid stock and big thoroughbrace. We present this view more to show what has been, for it is fast becoming a thing of the past.

MT. HOOD—Another mighty realism of God's handiwork in nature. In its towering grandeur it rises to a height of over eleven thousand feet.

PORTLAND, ambitious city of the far northwest, and metropolis of Oregon; city of fine architectural pretensions, and center of that magnificent grain-producing domain.

COLUMBIA RIVER, magnificent highway of commerce, grand in beautiful and impressive scenery.

THE NEEDLES OF THE COLUMBIA. In the elegant dining cars on this railroad you can feast on grand scenery and substantial viands at the same time.

YELLOWSTONE PARK—Vast and incomparable pleasure domain of the nation—three thousand five hundred and seventy-five square miles in area—a paradise of nature bordered by mountains of perpetual snow.

WHITE MOUNTAIN HOT SPRINGS—Nature's grand architectural skill in the white deposits, presenting the appearance of a frozen cascade, a rare sight. The overflowing of the calcareous springs and basins present the appearance of

TERRACES OF MANY TINTS—Scarlet, green, yellow, congealed against a snow-white ground of the steep hill sides. It defies description.

RIVERSIDE GEYSER—A column of boiling water, six feet in diameter, hurled by unseen might two hundred feet into the air; clouds of steam rising to one thousand feet. We next see

OLD FAITHFUL, which shoots her subterranean sea into the air every sixty-five minutes as regular as clock work, causing the earth to groan and tremble.

CONE OF LONE STAR GEYSER. Quiet and still where we can note with ease the undoubted evidences of past subterranean fires and volcanic forces.

CASTLE GEYSER—Bubbling, spouting, and erupting, throwing its tall transformation towers of boiling water high in the air.

UPPER FALLS OF THE YELLOWSTONE, where the foaming waters leap one hundred and forty feet down into the canyon, hissing in spray.

LOWER OR GREAT FALLS—The Yellowstone contracted by granite walls to within one hundred feet, rushes over a ledge in one wild, grand leap of three hundred and ninety-seven feet, a sheer compact, solid, perpendicular sheet of water.

GRAND CANYON—Its wall, one thousand five hundred feet in perpendicular height, and decorated in the most brilliant colors the eyes ever saw; weird-shaped, weather-worn rocks, a foaming, dashing, roaring torrent; grand depths, picturesque forms, unparalleled coloring.

TOWER FALLS, a cascade chastely beautiful, hidden away in the dim light of o'erhanging rocks and woods, its voice hushed to a murmur.

GIBBON FALLS. Here you have a view to stir the soul of an equestrian statue. This foaming cascade is best expressed in the word *grand*.

WHEAT-FIELDS IN DAKOTA as large as principalities on the continent. Kingdoms of agriculture in a single farm.

MINNEAPOLIS, the great flour city. The product of the great wheat-fields of Dakota is flowing daily through the hoppers of the famed

FLOURING MILLS of Minneapolis. There is enough flour made here daily to supply a city of forty-five thousand for a whole year.

ST. PAUL—Charming capital city of the great Minnesota state, beautiful executive buildings, splendid boulevards, winter sports, and

ICE PALACE. The ice palaces of St. Paul are the marvels of winter architecture, veritable castles with tower and turret and battlemented walls, glistening resplendent in the star-light walls of enchantment by illumination's glare.

MINNEHAHA FALLS ("Laughing Waters").

"And he journeyed without resting,
Till he heard the cataract's laughter,
Heard the Falls of Minnehaha
Calling to him through the silence:
'Pleasant is the sound,' he murmured,
'Of the lovely laughing Waters.'"

—*Longfellow.*

A glance at the waters of

LAKE SUPERIOR, an inland sea of fresh water, the largest in the world.

CHICAGO—Throbbing metropolis by Michigan's blue waters. No city in the world to compare with its lusty youth and mature commercial majesty. Young giant of the famed West. The famous

GRAIN ELEVATORS of Chicago are world renowned. They are the "barns" of the products of the fields of the great North-west.

As Chicago is the greatest railroad center in the world, we give a view of the

UNION DEPOT. There are upwards of eight hundred and fifty trains that arrive and depart from Chicago daily.

UNION STOCK-YARDS—Greatest in the world; the grand entrance;

INTERIOR VIEW—With marvellous accommodations; immense pens.

CINCINNATI. The Tyler Davidson Fountain, its sparkling flowing waters the daily delight of the proud Cincinnatian; a work of surpassing design; ideal fountain; a name perpetuated in water.

THE SUSPENSION BRIDGE—Aerial connecting link swung between Ohio and Kentucky; one of the most handsome bridges in the world; completed in 1866.

Prof. Morrow will here present the Art Gallery, embracing the latest portraits of American celebrities: Presidents, Statesmen, Warriors, Inventors, Authors, etc., forming a complete galaxy of the worthy men of note in the United States.

As Kentucky is the largest tobacco-producing state in the Union, we will here give a view of a

TOBACCO BARN, many of which may be seen while passing through this state. The world-famed blue grass region is near here, where the famous blooded

KENTUCKY HORSES are bred.

Glimpse of a Kentucky IDEAL.

THE MAMMOTH CAVE—Entrance low, dark, and uninviting, and the abode of bats. Of the

INTERIOR no pen can worthily portray and no picture fittingly reveal, still the camera accomplishes wonders.

INDIANAPOLIS—City of concentric circles; laid out after the manner of Washington City; great railroad center of twelve converging railroads; one hundred passenger trains go out daily.

DETROIT—Metropolis of Michigan, a charming city, with broad thoroughfares bordered by ornamenting shade-trees; delightful public "places," or parks; superior architecture.

CLEVELAND—By Erie's blue waters; city of broad thoroughfares and delighting umbrageous stretches; the Forest City; world-famed avenues and princely dwellings.

GREAT MOWER AND REAPER WORKS, where the farmer obtains the useful and ingenious machines for reducing his laborious toil.

CHAUTAUQUA—Great summer university, now enrolling the names of many thousand readers in literature, science, and religion.

THE AUDITORIUM in the grove will accommodate five thousand people, with a fine pipe organ. Here the best talent in the country appear during the summer months in concerts and lectures.

PORTRAIT OF LOUIS MILLER, one of the originators of Chautauqua University.

BISHOP J. H. VINCENT, Chancellor, whose leadership has made this institution a pronounced success.

YALE COLLEGE—Our proud pioneer institution of learning beneath the elms of New Haven; moved here from Saybrook in 1716; its old and honored halls still stand flanked by more ambitious modern structures.

BOSTON, "the Hub," panoramic view. The gilded State-house dome and wealth of magnificent buildings.

THE PUBLIC GARDENS of Boston, an addition to the famous Boston Commons, charming in parterres of flowers, winding walks, and sparkling fountains.

BUNKER HILL MONUMENT—Dear memorial to every American heart. Its plain shaft of gray granite, two hundred and twenty-one feet high, a grand milestone marking human freedom and progress.

OLD SOUTH CHURCH—Its homely pulpit and balcony and quaint furnishings; pew of Washington, it still presents a bold front to time.

We will now make a short visit to British America, first stopping at New Brunswick's metropolis,

ST. JOHNS—Strikingly situated on an elevated rocky peninsula; side fall of seventeen feet; two-thirds destroyed by fire in 1877; handsomely rebuilt.

HALIFAX, capital of Nova Scotia; of stucco and stone; the strong citadel; government house; St. Marys cathedral; fine air; beautiful scenery; famous as a watering-place.

QUEBEC, the "Gibraltar" of America, the most picturesque and most strongly fortified city on the continent; quaint and imposing architecture; great docks.

THE CITADEL—Remarkable fortifications; enchanting views from the ramparts; Dufferin terrace, magnificent promenade, one thousand four hundred feet long and two hundred above the river. A lingering spot for the sightseer.

View of the newly-erected

PARLIAMENTARY BUILDINGS, a royal pile of stone on the Grand Allée.

GLACIER STATION—The summit of the Canadian Pacific Railroad, four thousand feet above sea-level.

GLACIERS OF THE SELKIRKS. This phenomena of ice-rock and sunshine has existed for ages, and may justly be said to be the greatest glaciers on the face of the earth.

TORONTO—On lake Ontario; founded in 1794; a most pleasing city of broad streets, substantial buildings, and pleasant villas. Its magnificent university of Norman architecture, Trinity College of beautiful Gothic; a delightful city to linger in.

TOBOGGANING. The winter scenes and sports are the great attraction of this Northern metropolis in winter's icy night.

MIGHTY NIAGARA—Unparalleled reality of falling waters. Transfixed in awe and marvelling wonderment, one looks into the fearful gulf of Horse-shoe Falls, whose thunders roll up through driving, drenching mists. From the

MONTMORENCI FALLS, a beautiful sheet of o'erflowing waters; situate among the most romantic scenery on the globe.

MONTREAL—Chief city of the Dominion of Canada; built on a series of terraces; mountain side villas; Notre Dame Cathedral; the magnificent Victoria square.

SHOOTING THE RAPIDS. Pausing for a thrilling instant upon the brink of the dizzy current, the staunch steamer plunges into wildest confusion of foam-lashed waters swirling about the sunken rocks in fearful whirlpools and awful roar. The vessel careens and totters, but in another instant shoots out upon the calmer waters below. The world-famed

THOUSAND ISLANDS, gem-settings of nature upon the beautiful broad waters. The entranced eye feasts upon their umbrageous charms and picturesque shapes.

OTTAWA—Capital of the Dominion of Canada; of noble situation upon the beautiful Ottawa River, a new-made capital, its glory is its magnificent public buildings upon the rock-guarded banks.

SUSPENSION BRIDGE that spans the chasm like a thread, unsurpassed view is had of nature's watery veil glowing in delicate and tinted sheen.

Above the broad placid river, then a partial plunge, and the warring waters are hurried down the swift incline, and

THE RAPIDS are before you in awful hurry to you dread brinks where the crystallized waters leap into the eternal vale of cloud-mist with haunting roar and rumble.

Indescribable scenes of fantastic and fascinating beauty are found in the

ICE BRIDGES, which tempt the venturesome foot of the traveler.

How different

BY MOONLIGHT are the wondrous scenes about Niagara. The mysterious voices of night seem awakened, the mists arise from the troubled depths in fragments of grace and sweep to the star-depths above.

BUFFALO—Splendid city at the head of Lake Erie, possessing the
best and most capacious harbor on the lake; New York's third metropolis; magnificent city hall, costing $1,500,000; beautiful park of
six hundred and fifty-three acres.

A glimpse of the famous

OIL REGIONS of Pennsylvania, with landscape
honey-combed with borings, mammoth and un-
sightly derricks dotting the hills and valleys.

A most startling scene,

THE BURSTING OF A GAS-WELL, with flames
mounting heaven high, spreading wreck and devastation all about.

THE COAL MINING DISTRICTS possess a charm
for the inquiring tourist, and a sojourn among the
black diamond mines is fraught with instruction
and interest.

INCLINED RAILWAY. A view of the remarkable inclined railway at Mauch Chunk, Pennsylvania.

The heroic exploit of

BARBARA FRITCHIE will enthuse the patriot
of all ages. She could defy the deadly guns of
Jackson's men for love of the dear old flag.

> "Shoot, if you must, this old gray head,
> But spare your country's flag," she said.

BALTIMORE—Monumental City; the Peabody Institute; Washington Monument; Battle Monument; Johns Hopkins University;
said Park of seven hundred acres; city founded in 1729.

View of the

BROAD STREET STATION, PHILADELPHIA, one of the finest
modern depot buildings in the world.

THE NEW CITY BUILDINGS, now completing, occupying one
solid square, built of marble, with a magnificent tower surmounted
by a colossal statue of William Penn, thirty-five feet in height, the
whole mounting to five hundred and thirty-five feet.

INDEPENDENCE HALL—Cradle of liberty; built in 1735, and
contains some interesting historical relics.

INTERIOR, where the Declaration of Independence was
signed, showing the old table and Washington's chair.

GREAT SEWING MACHINE WORKS. This great industry has grown from a very small beginning until it is
now not only the largest industry in America, but the
greatest in the world.

CASTLE GARDEN, NEW YORK, the emigrant's gateway
to the paradise of a free country; the spot of Jenny Lind's
song triumphs; located at the Battery Park point, from whence a
sweeping view is had of New York's incomparable harbor.

WALL STREET, where the financial pulse of the nation too
fast beats with feverish anxiety; looking direct at old Trinity's
portals, with the Sub-treasury on the right, and banks and bro-
kers' offices of magnificent build and finish.

INSURANCE BUILDINGS—A view of the building containing
the offices of the greatest insurance company in existence, a rival to
the Bank of England.

New York's grand palace of mail, the $7,000,000

GENERAL POST OFFICE. Its marble walls present a triangu-
lar facade of tremendous architectural proportions. It is a commanding structure.

WINTER ON LUNA ISLAND

BUFFALO

OIL WELL PENNSYLVANIA

INCLINED RAILWAY MAUCH CHUNK

New York is famous for her fine breathing spots of greensward and flowers and fine trees, where one can find relief and rest, while the anxious throng hurries by; such is

UNION SQUARE, located at the head of Broadway, at 14th street. The ornate brown stone twin palace,

RESIDENCES OF THE VANDERBILTS, at Fifty-first street, fill the eye of the tourist with admiration.

ST. PATRICK'S CATHEDRAL. It is built of white marble, in the Gothic style, and is the most magnificent ecclesiastical structure built in our modern day. The delicate carving of its eastern facade and its elaborately traced windows rival the famed church structures of the Old World.

CENTRAL PARK—The beautiful fountain at the end of the mall on the plaza at the foot of the grand staircase. One of the creations of artistic beauty is

THE MARBLE BRIDGE, in Central Park.

THE OBELISK. An Old World wonder transplanted to the New World's shores is Cleopatra's Needle in Central Park, the gift of the Khedive of Egypt.

GRANT'S TOMB. The tomb of the hero of Appomattox, at Riverside, as it appeared on Decoration Day, decked with the floral tributes, sweet remembrances from a loving and revering people to the great captain.

GRAND CENTRAL DEPOT. The largest and finest railroad depot in America, at Forty-second street, New York, the eastern terminus of the great four-track Central Railway.

THE AMERICAN BIBLE HOUSE. The headquarters of Christian effort for the world's evangelization, at Ninth street, between Third and Fourth avenues. Here are printed Bibles in upwards of two hundred different languages.

We have now passed in review most of the famous places of interest on earth, and given some details of the features of each during our imaginary journey. Let me hope that the reader has added to his knowledge in perusing the descriptions, and experienced some pleasure and profit in viewing the enlarged photographs which this little book is intended to accompany.

What we have and said will, we hope, induce many to read and study the large book, which is described on the last inside cover page of this pamphlet.

GOOD NIGHT.

SONGS

INCIDENTAL TO

Dr. PHILIP PHILLIPS'

UNRIVALLED AND UNIQUE

ENTERTAINMENTS

AN APPROPRIATE SELECTION

From these popular Songs will be rendered each evening.
DURING the rendition of these Songs
MAGNIFICENT COLORED SCENES
will be crystalized before the eyes of the audience.
—THESE SCENES—
are of unusual Magnificence
—INTENSE in REALISM—
WHOLESOME in MORAL
REPLETE with STRIKING CHARACTER STUDIES
—AND STRONG—
in HUMAN INTEREST.

"*There remaineth a rest to the people of God.*"   PHILIP PHILLIPS.

1. I will sing you a song of that beau-ti-ful land, The far - a-way home of the soul; Where no storms ev-er beat on that glit-ter-ing strand, While the years of e-ter-ni-ty roll, roll. While the years of e-ter-ni-ty roll.

2 Oh, that home of the soul, in my visions and dreams,
Its bright jasper walls I can see,
Till I fancy but thinly the vale intervenes
Between the fair city and me.

3 There the great tree of life in its beauty doth grow,
And the river of life floweth by,
For no death ever enters that city, you know,
And nothing that maketh a lie.

4 That unchangeable home is for you and for me,
Where Jesus of Nazareth stands.
The King of all kingdoms forever is He,
And He holdeth our crowns in His hands.

5 Oh, how sweet it will be in that beautiful land,
So free from all sorrow and pain!
With songs on our lips, and with harps in our hands,
To meet one another again.

The above song is a specimen page taken from "SONG MINISTRY," a book which contains the Solos—seventy in all—as sung by Mr. Phillips, with piano and organ accompaniment. The songs are also richly illustrated and beautifully bound with his book of travels, entitled "SONG PILGRIMAGE."

ERRING ONE AND EVANGEL.

BISHOP I. W. WILEY.   *"Lay up for yourselves treasures in heaven."*   PHILIP PHILLIPS.

Tenor and Bass. Duett.

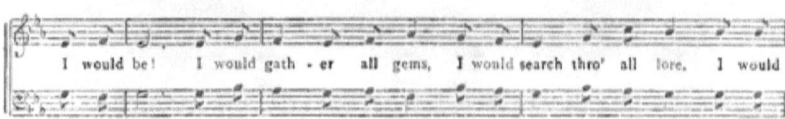

ERRING ONE.
If I had but the wealth of the world, E-van-gel, Oh, how hap-py a man

EVANGEL.
Have you thought of the rich-es of God, Err-ing One? Of the cit-y that's build-

I would be! I would gath-er all gems, I would search thro' all lore, I would

ed a-bove? Of the gems and the pearls, and the streets made of gold, Of the

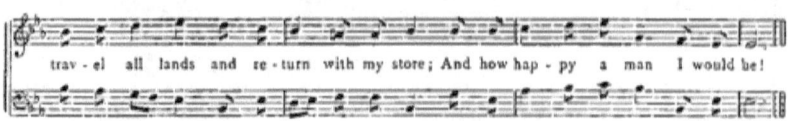

trav-el all lands and re-turn with my store; And how hap-py a man I would be!

beau-ties and glo-ries whose wealth is un-told, That are kept for the saints of His love?

ERRING ONE.   I would build me a mansion of stone, Evangel,
       Out of gems, clear and polished like glass;
       I'd surround it with lawns, and with trees and with flowers,
       With rich statues, pure streams, and with green rosy bowers,
       Such as nothing on earth could surpass.

EVANGEL.   Have you thought of the mansions of God, Erring One,
       Which He builds for His children on high?
       Can you build as can He who hath made the great world?
       Or adorn as can He who the sky hath unfurled,
       And whose bounties all creatures supply?

ERRING ONE.   I would fill it with pictures, and purchase rare wines;
       I'd surround me with children and friends;
       And with music and song, and with dance would be gay,
       And would fear for no want and would dread no decay,
       And my pleasures would never have end.

EVANGEL.   Have you thought how earth's riches take wings, Erring One—
       How our children and friends pass away;
       How the strong man grows weak, and how pleasures grow stale,
       Or how beauty soon fades, or our senses soon fail,
       As we haste to that infinite day?

ERRING ONE.   I would seek the world's honors, and make me a name;
EVANGEL.   But your honor and fame would soon die!
ERRING ONE.   Can I claim nothing, then, Evangel, as my own?
EVANGEL.   If you had all the world, nothing's yours, Erring One;
       All is His who doth reign in the sky.

ERRING ONE.   Can I have, then, these riches of God, Evangel,
       That honor those mansions above?
EVANGEL.   God hath made them for you, and for me, and for all,
BOTH.   Who before Him in faith, love, and duty will fall,
       He will raise to the bliss of His love.

Rearranged from "Singing Pilgrim," and copyrighted by Philip Phillips, 1887.

ETERNAL LIFE, MY CRY.

"Lay hold on eternal life."

PHILIP PHILLIPS.

Would'st thou be saved? No time to lose: A - rise, and run the heav'n - ly road. Would'st

thou be blest? Then, Pil-grim, haste to leave destruction's dread a-bode, Oh come, (Oh come,) the

Sav - iour calls, "I am the Way, the Truth, the Life; Come hith - er, burdened soul, to Me."

PILGRIM.

Oh, tell me how! Oh, tell me where!
The way I long have sought to know;
But fear the guilt and sin I bear
Will sink me in the depths of woe.

EVANGELIST.

God's word will guide thee: dost thou see
A light from yonder distant hill?
On, Pilgrim, on! it shines for thee;
With steady course pursue it still. *Chorus.*

PILGRIM.

God's word will guide me; yes, I see
A light from yonder distant hill;
Oh, tell me, does it shine for me?
Hail, glorious light! I will, I will!

PILGRIM AND EVANGELIST.

Farewell, a long farewell to those
Who seek to stay me as I fly;
My ears against their call I close,
Life, life, eternal life! my cry. *Chorus.*

Copyrighted by Philip Phillips, in "Singing Pilgrim," 1865.

PERSUASIVE VOICE.

"And I beheld, and heard an angel flying through the midst of heaven."

PHILIP PHILLIPS.

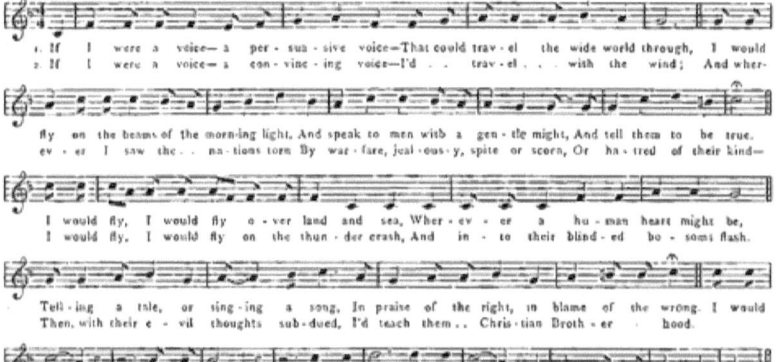

1. If I were a voice—a per - sua - sive voice—That could trav - el the wide world through, I would
2. If I were a voice— a con - vinc - ing voice—I'd trav - el . . . with the wind; And wher-

fly on the beams of the morn-ing light, And speak to men with a gen - tle might, And tell them to be true.
ev - er I saw the . . na - tions torn By war - fare, jeal - ous - y, spite or scorn, Or ha - tred of their kind—

I would fly, I would fly o - ver land and sea, Wher - ev - er a hu - man heart might be,
I would fly, I would fly on the thun - der crash, And in - to their blind - ed bo - soms flash.

Tell - ing a tale, or sing - ing a song, In praise of the right, in blame of the wrong. I would
Then, with their e - vil thoughts sub - dued, I'd teach them . . Chris - tian Broth - er - hood.

fly, I would fly, I would fly o - ver land and sea, o - ver land and sea.

3 If I were a voice—a consoling voice—
 I'd fly on the wings of the air;
 The homes of sorrow and guilt I'd seek,
 And calm and truthful words I'd speak,
 To save them from despair.
 I would fly, I would fly o'er the crowded town,
 And drop like the happy sunlight, down
 Into the hearts of suffering men,
 And teach them to look up again.
 :¦: I would fly :¦: o'er the crowded town.

4 If I were a voice—an immortal voice—
 I would fly the earth around;
 And wherever man to his idols bowed,
 I'd publish in notes both long and loud,
 The Gospel's joyful sound.
 I would fly, I would fly on the wings of day,
 Proclaiming peace on my world-wide way,
 Bidding the saddened earth rejoice,
 If I were a voice—an immortal voice—
 :¦: I would fly :¦: on the wings of day.

SONG OF SALVATION.

"For God so loved the world that He gave his only-begotten Son."   PHILIP PHILLIPS.

1. I have heard of a Saviour's love, And a won-der-ful love it must be; But did He come down from a-
2. I have heard how he suffer'd and bled, How He languish'd and died on the tree; But then is it a - ny where
3. I've been told of a heav'n on high, Which the children of Je - sus shall see; But is there a place in the
4. Lord, answer these questions of mine, To whom shall I go but to Thee? And say by Thy Spir-it di-

bove, Out of love and com-pas-sion for me, for me, Out of love and com-pas-sion for me!
said, That He languish'd and suf-fer'd for me, for me, That He languish'd and suf-fer'd for me?
sky, Made read - y and furnish'd for me, for me, Made read - y and fur-nish'd for me?
vine, There's a Sav-iour and heav-en for me, for me, There's a Sav-iour and heav-en for me.

SCRIPTURE RESPONSE TO VERSE 1.   SCRIPTURE RESPONSE TO VERSE 2.

It is a faithful saying, | that Christ Jesus | He was wounded for our transgres-
and worthy of . . | all ac-cep-ta-tion, | came into the . | world to save sinners. | sions, He was bruised for . .

our in - | iquities; the chastisement of our peace was up - on Him; and with His stripes we are healed.

SCRIPTURE RESPONSE TO VERSE 3.

In my Father's house are ma - ny man-sions; | If it were not so I would have told | place for you; that
you. I go to prepare a . . . . |

CHORUS—*to last verse only.*

where I am ye may be al - so. Yes, yes, yes, for me, for me, Yes, yes, yes, for me;

Ritard.

Our Lord from a - bove in his in - fi - nite love, On the cross died to save you and me.

THE PARDON.

"Let him return unto the Lord. . . . He will abundantly pardon."   PHILIP PHILLIPS.

Slow and distinct.   *Soft.*

Cold and bleak the winds were blowing, Faint - ly toll'd the midnight bell, Sad - ly moan'd a wretched cap-tive,

In his lone-ly pris-on cell; Pac - ing wild ly, pac - ing wild-ly Up and down his pris - on cell.

Cres.

Thought had nerv'd his soul to mad-ness, Hear the clinking of his chain. He would rend its links a - sun - der,

Largo.

But the strug-gle is in vain. Helpless vic - tim, helpless vic-tim, Crime had forg'd that heavy chain.

Light and staccato.

{ Home—he starts with fear and trembles, Hides his face with guilt and shame; }
{ Moth - er—hush! he dare not breathe it! Dare not speak that hal-lowed name. } Let his anguish, let his anguish,

One bright tear of pity claim. | Sentenced from | He must meet | Soon for him
the bar of . . | Justice, | a convict's | doom. | will dawn the | morrow, Veil'd in clouds of awful

Dim.

gloom; Growing deep-er, growing deep-er, As he nears the sol-emn tomb. Now the fa - tal hour ap-proach-es,

Very slow.   *pp*

Hark! the jailer's measured tread; One brief moment, all is ready, To the scaffold he is led. They have drawn it,

THE PARDON. Concluded.

they have drawn it, Drawn the black cap o'er his head. "Loose the prisoner!" All is si-lent. With his head erect and proud,

Comes a foaming steed, all breathless, Dashing thro' the wond'ring crowd;
And his rid - er, and his rid - er Waves his hand, and cries aloud: "Loose the prisoner! Loose him quickly!

He is pardoned, free as air! I have hastened with the message, Look! his par - don now I bear!"

Thus in mer - cy, thus in mer - cy, God the sin - ner deigns to spare, When a - gainst His laws re - bel-ling,
Mer - cy plead-ing, mer-cy pleading, Shines a sun-beam o'er the gloom; Love, e - ter - nal love, enfolds him,

Jus - tice seals his fear - ful doom; Shuts from him the light of glo - ry, Brings him al - most to the tomb.
Je - sus brings a sweet re-prieve; Pre - cious par - don, free and boundless, All who ask it may re-ceive.

FATHER, TAKE MY HAND.

"Commit thy way unto the Lord." Written for Mr. PHILLIPS, by S. J. VAIL.

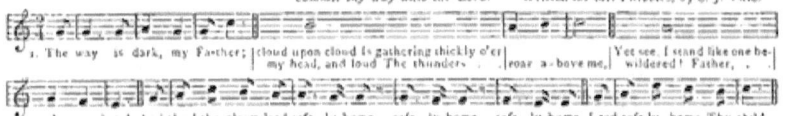

1. The way is dark, my Father; cloud upon cloud is gathering thickly o'er my head, and loud The thunders roar a-bove me, Yet see, I stand like one be-wildered! Father, . .

take my hand, And thro' the gloom lead safe - ly home, safe - ly home, safe - ly home, Lead safely home Thy child.

2. The day declines, my Father! | and the night
Is drawing darkly down. My faithless sight
Sees | ghostly | visions. | Fears of a spectral band
Encompass me. O Father, | take my | hand,
And from the night lead up to light,
Up to light, up to light,
Lead up to light Thy child.

3. The way is long, my Father: | and my soul
Longs for the rest and quiet | of the | goal; |
While yet I journey through this weary land,
Keep me from wandering. Father, | take my | hand,
And in the way to endless day,
Endless day, endless day,
Lead safely on Thy child.

4. The path is rough, my Father! | many a thorn
Has pierced me; and my feet, all torn
And bleeding, | mark the | way. | Yet Thy command
Bids me press forward. Father, | take my | hand,
Then safe and blest, oh, lead to rest,
Lead to rest, lead to rest,
Oh, lead to rest Thy child.

5. The cross is heavy, Father! | I have borne
It long, and | still do | bear it. | Let my worn
And fainting spirit rise to that bright land
Where crowns are given. Father, | take my | hand,
And, reaching down, lead to the crown,
To the crown, to the crown,
Lead to the crown Thy child.

CODA FOR LAST VERSE.

The way is dark, my child, but leads to light; I would not al - ways have thee walk by sight; My destinies now thou

canst not understand; I mean it so, but I will take thy hand, And thro' the gloom Lead safely home, Lead safely home my **child**.

THE GRAND OLD STORY.

"Now all this was done, that it might be fulfilled which was spoken of the Lord by the prophet."
Words by DR. H. BONAR. PHILIP PHILLIPS.

1. Come, and hear the grand old sto - ry, Sto - ry of the a - ges past, All earth's an-nals far sur - pass-ing,
2. Christ, the Father's Son e - ter - nal, Once was born a Son of man; He, who never knew be - gin-ning,

REFRAIN. Ritard. A tempo.

Sto - ry that shall ev - er last. Noblest, Truest, Oldest, Newest, Saddest, Gladdest, That this world has ev-er known.
Here, on earth, a life be - gan.

3. Words of truth and deeds of kindness,
Miracles of grace and might,
Scatter fragrance all around Him,
Shine with heaven's most glorious light.
In Gethsemane behold Him,
In the agony of prayer;
Kneeling, pleading, groaning, bleeding,
Soul and body prostrate there.

5. On to Golgotha he hastens,
Yonder stands His cross of woe:
From the hands, and feet, and forehead,
See the precious life-blood flow.
6. It is finished! see his body
Laid alone in Joseph's tomb;
'Tis for us He lieth yonder,
Prince of Life, enwrapped in gloom.

7. But in vain the grave has bound Him,
Death has barred its gates in vain;
See, for us the Saviour rises,
Lo! for us He bursts the chain.
8. Hear we, then, this grand old story,
And, in listening, learn to love;
Flowing through it to the guilty
From a pardoning God above.

9

GUARD THY TONGUE.

"The tongue is a little member, and boasteth great things."

PHILIP PHILLIPS.

1. Guard the tongue, and guard it wise-ly, Thence a world of e-vil springs; Though it be a lit-tle mem-ber, Yet it boast-eth won-drous things. It can whis-per words of com-fort; It can wound and cheer the heart; It can seal the bonds of u-nion; It can break them all a-part.

2. It can cheer the sad and lone-ly, Like a beam of morn-ing light; O'er a gen-tle, lov-ing spir-it, It can throw a cru-el blight. We have need to guard it wise-ly, And be care-ful what we say, Lest we harm an err-ing brother, Who may stum-ble by the way.

CHORUS. *Largo.* ... *Ritard.*

"Set a watch, O Lord, be-fore my mouth, And keep Thou the door of my lips."

3. With the tongue we blend our voices
In the melody of song;
With the tongue we utter falsely,
And we do each other wrong.
Can a single fountain give us
Sweet and bitter waters too!
Yes! the tongue speaks good and evil,
Though it ought not so to do.
Set a watch, &c.

4. How a spark of angry feeling
It will kindle to a flame;
We can chain the savage lion,
But the tongue can no man tame.
With the tongue we bless our Father,
With the tongue His law profane,
With the tongue we praise our Maker,
And we take His Name in vain.
CODA.—For of every kind of beasts, &c.

5. Hush that idle whisper, sister,
Think the Lord is standing near,
Listening to each word thou speakest
Of the souls to Him so dear!
Tell how firmly walks thy brother;
All his brave and true deeds tell;
Speak not of the past's dark errors,
Tell not that he tripped and fell.
Set a watch, &c.

Coda to fourth verse.

"For of ev-'ry kind of beasts, and of birds, and of serpents, and things in the sea is tamed, But the tongue can no man tame. Therewith we bless God, e-ven the Fa-ther; and therewith we curse men in God's im-age made; Out of the same mouth blessings and cursings. My brethren, these things ought not so to be."

CHORUS.

LEAP FOR LIFE.

GEO. P. MORRIS.

"Obey your parents."

HENRY RUSSELL.

Old I-ron-sides at an-chor lay In the har-bor of Ma-hon; A dead calm rest-ed on the bay, The waves to sleep had gone; When lit-tle Hal, the captain's son, A lad, both brave and good, In sport, up shroud and rig-ging ran, And on the main-truck stood. A shudder shot thro' ev-'ry vein, All eyes were turned on high; There stood the boy, with diz-zy brain, Be-tween the sea and sky. No hold had he a-bove—be-low— A-lone he stood in air; At that far height none dared to go, At that far height none dared to go, No aid could reach him there. We gazed, but not a man could speak; With horror all a-ghast, In groups with pal-lid brow and cheek, We watched the quiv'ring mast. The atmosphere was dim and hot, And of a lu-rid hue, As riv-et-ed un-to the spot, Stood of-fi-cers and crew. We gazed, but not a man could speak; We

LEAP FOR LIFE. Concluded.

gazed, but not a man could speak, Not a man could speak. The father came on deck—He gasped—O God, thy will be

done! Then sud-den-ly a ri-fle grasped, And aimed it at his son. Jump far out, boy, in-to the wave!

Jump, or I fire, he said; That on-ly chance your life can save. Jump, jump, boy! He o-beyed. He sank,— he

rose,— he lived,— he moved,— He for the ship struck out; On board we hail the lad we love, On

board we hail the lad we love, On board we hail the lad we love, On board we hail the lad we love, On

board we hail the lad we love, With man-y and man-y a man-ly shout. His fa-ther drew, in

si-lent joy, Those wet arms round his neck, Then fold-ed to his heart the boy, And faint-ed on the deck.

HOME PATRIOTISM.

FANNY CROSBY.   *"A land that floweth with milk and honey."*   PHILIP PHILLIPS.

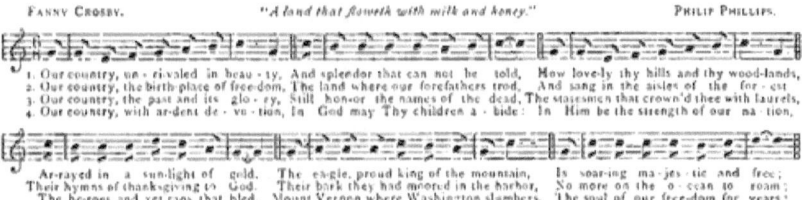

1. Our country, un-ri-valed in beau-ty, And splendor that can not be told, How love-ly thy hills and thy wood-lands,
2. Our country, the birth-place of free-dom, The land where our forefathers trod, And sang in the aisles of the for-est
3. Our country, the past and its glo-ry, Still honor the names of the dead, The statesmen that crown'd thee with laurels,
4. Our country, with ar-dent de-vo-tion, In God may Thy children a-bide: In Him be the strength of our na-tion.

Ar-rayed in a sun-light of gold. The ea-gle, proud king of the mountain, Is soar-ing ma-jes-tic and free;
Their hymns of thanksgiving to God. Their bark they had moored in the harbor, No more on the o-cean to roam;
The he-roes and vet-rans that bled. Mount Vernon where Washington slumbers, The soul of our free-dom for years;
His laws and His counsel its guide. Our banner—that time-honored ban-ner That floats o'er the ocean's bright foam—

Thy rivers and lakes in their grandeur, Roll on to the arms of the sea, . . Roll on to the arms of the sea.
And there, in the wilds of New England, They founded a country and home, . They founded a country and home,
A willow droops ten-der-ly o'er him, Go hal-low his grave with thy tears, . Go hal-low his grave with thy tears.
God keep them unsullied for-ev-er, Our standard, our union, our home, . Our standard, our union, our home.

RENOUNCE THE CUP.

"Nor thieves, nor drunkards shall inherit the kingdom of God."   ARR. by PHILIP PHILLIPS.

RECITATIVE.

1. A drunk-ard reached his cheer-less home, The storm with-out was dark and wild; He forced his
2. And cold-er still the winds did blow, And dark-er hours of night came on, And deep-er

weep-ing wife to roam, A wan-d'rer, friend-less, with her child. As thro' the fall-ing
grew the drift-ed snow, Her limbs were chilled, her strength was gone. O God! she cried, in

snow she pressed, The babe was sleep-ing on her breast, The babe was sleep-ing on her breast,
ne-cents wild, If I must per-ish, save my child, If I must per-ish, save my child.

3 She stripped the mantle from her breast,
And bared her bosom to the storm,
As round the child she wrapped the vest,
She smiled to think that it was warm.
With one cold kiss, a tear of grief,
The broken-hearted found relief.

4 At morn her cruel husband passed,
And saw her on her snowy bed;
Her tearful eyes were closed at last,
Her cheek was pale, her spirit fled.
He raised the mantle from the child,
The babe looked up, and sweetly smiled.

5 Shall this sad warning plead in vain !
Poor thoughtless one, *it speaks to you;*
Now break the tempter's cruel chain,
No more your dreadful way pursue :
Renounce the cup, to Jesus fly—
Immortal soul, why will you die ?

SCATTER SEEDS OF KINDNESS.

"To him that soweth righteousness, shall be a sure reward."

Mrs. A. Smith.   Written for Mr. Phillips by S. J. Vail.

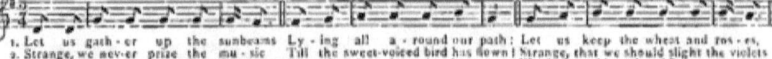

1. Let us gath-er up the sunbeams Ly-ing all a-round our path; Let us keep the wheat and ros-es,
2. Strange, we nev-er prize the mu-sic Till the sweet-voiced bird has flown; Strange, that we should slight the violets
3. If we knew the ba-by fin-gers, Pressed against the win-dow pane, Would be cold and still to-mor-row—
4. Ah! those lit-tle ice-cold fin-gers, How they point our memories back To the has-ty words and ac-tions

Cast-ing out the thorns and chaff; Let us find our sweet-est com-fort In the bless-ings of to-day,
Till the love-ly flowers are gone! Strange, that summer skies and sun-shine Nev-er seem one-half so fair,
Nev-er trouble us a-gain— Would the bright eyes of our dar-ling Catch the frown up-on our brow?
Strewn a-long our backward track! How those lit-tle hands re-mind us, As in snow-y grace they lie,

CHORUS.

With a pa-tient hand re-mov-ing All the bri-ars from the way,
As when win-ter's snow-y pin-ions Shake the white down in the air. Then scatter seeds of kindness,
Would the print of ros-y fin-gers Vex us then as they do now?
Not to scat-ter thorns—but roses— For our reap-ing by and by!

Then scat-ter seeds of kindness, Then scat-ter seeds of kindness, For our reaping by and by.

NO TEARS IN HEAVEN.

"There shall be no more death, neither sorrow, nor crying."   Wm. B. Bradbury.

RECITATIVE.

1. I met a child, his feet were bare, His weak frame . . shivered with the cold; It is youthful brow was knit with care, His flashing must we part," he cried, "so soon!" As down his . . . eye his sor-row told.
2. I saw a man in life's gay noon, Stand weeping . . o'er his young bride's bier; "And . . . cheek there rolled a tear.

Said I, "Poor boy, why weep-est thou?" "My parents are both dead," he said, "I have not where to lay my head;
"Heart-stricken one," said I, "weep not!" "Weep not!" in accent wild he cried, "But yes-ter-day my loved one died,

Soothingly.

Oh! I am lone and friendless now." "Not friendless, child, a Friend on high, For you His pre-cious
And shall she be so soon for-got?" "For-got-ten? no! still let her love Sus-tain thy heart, with

blood has given; Cheer up, and bid each tear be dry, There are no tears, no tears in heaven."
an-guish riven; Strive thou to meet thy bride a-bove, And dry your tears, your tears in heaven."

3. I saw a gentle mother weep,
As to her throbbing heart she pressed
An infant, seemingly asleep
On its kind mother's sheltering breast.
"Fair one," said I, "pray weep no more."
Sobbed she, "The idol of my hope
I now am called to render up;
My babe has reach'd death's gloomy shore."

"Young mother, yield no more to grief,
Nor be by passion's tempest driven,
But find in these sweet words relief,
There are no tears, no tears in heaven."

4. Poor traveler o'er life's troubled wave—
Cast down by grief, o'erwhelmed by care—
There is an arm above can save,
Then yield not thou to fell despair.

Look upward, mourners, look above!
What though the thunders echo loud,
The sun shines bright above the cloud;
Then trust to thy Redeemer's love.
Where'er thy lot in life be cast,
Whate'er of toil or woe be given,
Be firm; remember to the last,
"There are no tears, no tears in heaven."

THE THREE WARNINGS.

"Awake, thou that sleepest."   I. B. Woodbury (newly arranged.)

Allegretto.

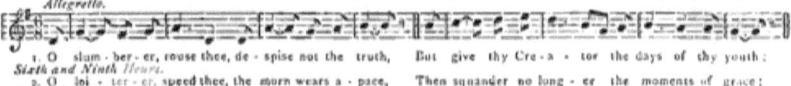

1. O slum-ber-er, rouse thee, de-spise not the truth, But give thy Cre-a-tor the days of thy youth;
Sixth and Ninth Hours.
2. O loi-ter-er, speed thee, the morn wears a-pace, Then squander no long-er the moments of grace;
Eleventh and Last Hours.
3. O sin-ner, a-rouse thee, the morn-ing is past, Al-read-y the shad-ows are length-en-ing fast;

Why stand-est there i-dle, the day breaketh, the The Lord of the Vine-yard is wait-ing for thee.
But haste while there's time, with thy Mas-ter a-gree, The Lord of the Vineyard stands waiting for thee.
Es-cape for thy life, from the dark mountains flee, The Lord of the Vine-yard is wait-ing for thee.

THE THREE WARNINGS. Concluded.

Pleading. p

Ho - ly Spir - it, by Thy power, Grant me yet an - oth - er hour; Earthly pleasures I would prove,
Gen - tle Spir - it, stay, oh, stay! Brightly beams the ear - ly day; Let me lin - ger in these bowers,
Spir - it, cease Thy mournful lay; Leave me to my - self, I pray. Earth hath flung her spell a - round me.

Ritard.

Earth-ly joy and earth - ly love; Scarcely yet has dawn'd the day, Ho - ly Spir - it, wait, I pray.
God shall have my noon - tide hours, Chide me not for my de - lay; Gen - tle Spir - it, wait, I pray.
Pleasure's silk - en chain hath bound me; When the sun has path hath trod, Spir - it, then I'll turn to God!

KNELL—*for last verse. Allegretto.*

Hark! borne on the wind is the bell's sol - emn toll, 'Tis mourn - ful - ly peal - ing the knell of a soul;

The Spir - it's sweet pleadings and strivings are o'er, The Lord of the Vineyard Stands wait-ing no more.

THE NINETY AND NINE.

E. C. CLEPHANE.   *"Rejoice with Me, for I have found My sheep."*   IRA D. SANKEY.

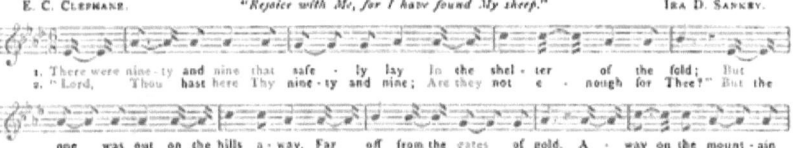

1. There were nine - ty and nine that safe - ly lay In the shel - ter of the fold; But
2. "Lord, Thou hast here Thy nine - ty and nine; Are they not e - nough for Thee?" But the

one was out on the hills a - way, Far off from the gates of gold, A - way on the mount - ain
Shepherd made an - swer: "This of Mine Has wan - dered a - way from Me; And al - though the road be

wild and bare, A - way from the Shepherd's ten - der care, A - way from the Shepherd's ten - der care
rough and steep, I go to the desert to find My sheep, I go to the desert to find my sheep."

3 But none of the ransomed ever knew
 How deep were the waters crossed;
Nor how dark was the night that the Lord passed through,
 Ere He found His sheep that was lost.
Out of the desert He heard its cry—
'Twas helpless and sick, and ready to die.

4 And all through the mountains, thunder-riven,
 And up from the rocky steep,
There rose a cry to the gate of heaven,
 "Rejoice! I have found My sheep."
And the angels echoed around the throne,
 "Rejoice, for the Lord brings back His own!"

BY-GONE DAYS.

1. I've wan - dered to the vil - lage, Tom, I've sat be - neath the tree Up - on the school-house
2. The grass is just as green, dear Tom; bare - foot - ed boys at play Were sporting there as
3. That old school-house has al - tered some; the bench - es are re - placed By new ones ver - y
4. The riv - e'rs run - ning just as still; the wil - lows on its side Are lar - ger than they

play - ground, which shel - tered you and me; But none were there to greet me, Tom, and
we did then, with spir - its just as gay; But the mas - ter sleeps up - on the hill, which
like the ones our pen - knives had de - faced; The same old bricks are in the wall, the
were, dear Tom; the stream ap - pears less wide; The grape - vine swing is ru - ined now, where

Rall.

few were left to know, That played with us up on the grass, some twen - ty years a - go.
coat - ed o'er with snow, Af - ford - ed us a slid - ing place, just twen - ty years a - go.
bell swings to and fro, The mu - sic just the same, dear Tom, 'twas twen - ty years a - go.
once we played the beau, And swung our sweet-hearts—pret - ty girls!—just twen - ty years a - go.

5 The spring that bubbled 'neath the hill, close by the springing beach,
Is very low—'twas once so high that we could almost reach ;—
And kneeling down to get a drink, dear Tom, I started so !
To find that I had changed so much since twenty years ago.

6 The boys were playing the same old game, beneath the same old tree—
I do forget the name just now,) you've played the same with me
On that same spot ;—'twas played with knives, by throwing to and so ;—
The leader had a task to do, there, twenty years ago.

7 Down by the spring, upon an elm, you know I cut your name,
Your sweetheart's just beneath it, Tom,—and you did mine the same ;

Some heartless wretch has peeled the bark,—'twas dying sure, but slow,
Just as the one whose name was cut died, twenty years ago.

8 My lids have long been dry, dear Tom, but tears came to my eyes—
I thought of those we loved so well—those early broken ties ;
I visited the old church-yard, and took some flowers to strew
Upon the graves of those we loved, some twenty years ago.

9 Some are in the church-yard laid, some sleep beneath the sea ;—
But few are left of our old class excepting you and me ;
And when our time shall come, dear Tom, and we are called to go,
I hope they'll lay me where we played just twenty years ago.

GOSPEL HEROES.

PHILIP PHILLIPS.

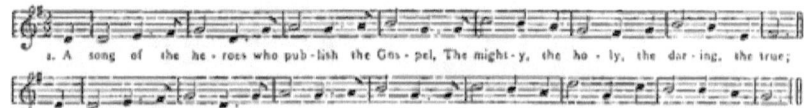

1. A song of the he-roes who pub-lish the Gos-pel, The might-y, the ho-ly, the dar-ing, the true;

A song for God's chil-dren who serve him sin-cere-ly, Is one which I now shall be sing-ing to you.

2 With reverence to age we must first mention Beecher,
Whom all will acknowledge the great Brooklyn preacher
Most able, persuasive, outspoken, and free,
He speaks his convictions though none may agree

3 With temperance we think of John Gough the reformer
Who fearlessly faces the foe in the fight;
Unequaled in pathos, a peerless example,
We sing forth his praises in battling for right.

4 Next comes Doctor Talmage, the tried and the true,
Whose powers of description are graphic and new;
His sermons in all of the nations are found,
His talents most rare and his preaching renowned.

5 Of Cook we now sing as the man for our time,
His logic he thunders in accents sublime;
The skeptical world is now trembling with fear,
While Christians rejoice with fresh courage and cheer.

6 There's pleasure in singing of dear Doctor Vincent,
Most highly esteemed by young and by old;
His rare Christian culture, Chautauqua unfurled—
Proclaim him the prince of the Sunday School world.

7 In song we will tell of our dear Brother Moody,
Whose power is from heaven in preaching the word;
His Master has called him to work in his vineyard,
In leading great masses to Christ in this age.

8 Most gladly we sing of the great English preacher,
Charles Spurgeon, of London, so good and so wise;
Proclaiming the truth as it is in Christ Jesus,
So clearly with unction received from the skies.

CHORUS—*to be sung with the audience after the last verse.*
May God in his mercy still help them to labor,
And hold up the cross in its grandeur sublime;
Oh, long may they stand as the watchmen of Zion,
God bless and reward them—the men of our time.

YOUR MISSION.

MRS. E. H. GATES.   *(As sung by Mr. Phillips at the request of President Lincoln.)*   S. M. GRANNIS.

1. If you can not on the o-cean Sail a-mong the swift-est fleet, Rock-ing on the high-est bil-lows,
2. If you are too weak to journey Up the mount-ain, steep and high, You can stand with-in the val-ley,
3. If you have not gold and sil-ver Ev-er read-y to command; If you can not 'twards the need-y

Laugh-ing at the storms you meet; You can stand a-mong the sail-ors, An-chor'd yet with-in the bay,
While the mul-ti-tudes go by; You can chant in hap-py meas-ure, As they slow-ly pass a-long,
Reach an ev-er-o-pen hand; You can vis-it the af-flict-ed, O'er the err-ing you can weep,

You can lend a hand to help them, As they launch their boats a-way, As they launch their boats a-way.
Tho' they may for-get the sing-er, They will not for-get the song, They will not for-get the song.
You can be a true dis-ci-ple, Sit-ting at the Sav-iour's feet, Sit-ting at the Sav-iour's feet.

4 If you can not in the conflict
Prove yourself a soldier true,
If, where fire and smoke are thickest,
There's no work for you to do;
When the battle-field is silent,
You can go with careful tread,
You can bear away the wounded,
You can cover up the dead.

5 If you can not in the harvest
Garner up the richest sheaves,
Many a grain both ripe and golden
Will the careless reapers leave;
Go and glean among the briars,
Growing rank against the wall,
For it may be that their shadow
Hides the heaviest wheat of all.

6 Do not, then, stand idly waiting
For some greater work to do;
Fortune is a lazy goddess,
She will never come to you.
Go, and toil in any vineyard,
Do not fear to do or dare;
If you want a field of labor,
You can find it any where.

I WILL SING FOR JESUS.

"Singing and making melody in your heart to the Lord."   PHILIP PHILLIPS.

SOLO.

1. I will sing for Je-sus, With His blood He bought me, And all a-long my
2. Can there o-ver-take me, A-ny dark dis-as-ter, While I sing for
3. I will sing for Je-sus! His name a-lone pre-vail-ing, Shall be my sweet-est

CHORUS.

pil-grim way His lov-ing hand has brought me.
Je-sus, My bless-ed, bless-ed Mas-ter? O, help me sing for Je-sus,
mu-sic, When heart and flesh are fail-ing.

Help me tell the sto-ry Of Him who did re-deem us, The Lord of life and glo-ry.

THE POWER OF TRUTH.

"Lying lips are abomination to the Lord."

PHILLIPS and GOUGH.

The bell had ceased, the an-chor weighed, And proud-ly on her way, See yon-der state-ly ves-sel ride

A-mid the dash-ing spray; And faint-er now the dis-tant view Of spire and loft-y dome,

That leaves to mem'ry and the soul The last fond look of home, The last fond look of home. But

who that slen-der boy that stands, With cheeks so wan and pale, Be-fore the stern, re-lent-less mate,

And tells his sim-ple tale? Be-neath that keen, re-proachful glance, His eye is calm and clear, "You

found me in the hold," he said, "My fa-ther left me there." "'Tis false, 'tis false," the mate re-plied, and

thrust the boy a-way, To hear his cold and cru-el words,—And feel his cru-el sway. But

truth un-daunt-ed bore the test, It would not yield to fear; The boy per-sist-ing still declared,

"My fa-ther left me there."— "You shall be conquered," cried the mate; "I'll make you yield at last.

Now tell the truth, or hear me, boy, You'll swing from yon-der mast." He dragg'd him to the crowded deck,

And stood with watch in hand. "Two min-utes more; come, come, be quick." He called, with stern com-mand.

He crossed the deck, then paused to hear His help-less vic-tim say, "I told the truth, and on-ly ask

One mo-ment, sir, to pray. One mo-ment, sir, to pray." Those lift-ed hands, that

an-gel face, Ah, who unmoved could see? "Now, dear Fa-ther, heav'nly Fa-ther, Come and take me

home to Thee." A-mid con-vul-sive, pit-ying sobs, That could not be suppressed,

The mate sprang for-ward, caught the child, And strained him to his breast. "Live, live," he cried, "and

may I learn From thee, my no-ble youth, To love my God, who taught thy heart The

law of sa-cred truth; To love my God, who taught thy heart The law of sa-cred truth."

SINGING 'ROUND THE WORLD.

PHILIP PHILLIPS

1. You who love the grand-eur of the vast cre-a-tion, Lis-ten to a sto-ry wo-ven in a song,
Trac-ing in their splendour scenes that rose before us, Round the world of won-ders while we pass a-long.
Start-ing on our jour-ney from the Em-pire Cit-y, Of its wealth and commerce vol-umes we could say ;.....
But to Phil-a-del-phia, where the bell of free-dom Rang our in-de-pend-ence on that "glo-rious day."

2 O'er the South we journey, o'er its sunny regions,
Drinking in its beauties—what delight is ours !
With its vernal landscapes Florida beguiles us,
Florida our fathers called the land of flowers ;
Stately pines are waving in the laughing breeze,
Golden fruits are dropping from the orange trees ;
All around is smiling, all of joy is telling,
Every thing to charm us, every thing to please,

3 O'er the Mississippi and the great Missouri
We have glided onward 'neath the sky so blue ;
At the grave of Lincoln, sacred to our nation,
Saviour of our country, faithful, loyal, true ;
Over California, where for days we journeyed,
Pleasant were the changes, rich in beauty rare ;
But Yosemite Valley rivals all description,
With its falls majestic and their rainbows fair.

4 Thro' a park we journey, speeding out before us
Like a panorama—Yellowstone its name ;
See the geyser fountains into air ascending !
Then again receding quickly as they came.
Farms of finest culture, fields of growing wheat,
Orchards, too, and meadows all around we meet ;
While the honest farmer, resting from his labor,
Smiles upon the children gathered at his feet.

5 Australia, England, Scotland, Erin, famed in story,
Holland, France, Italia, where the poets dwell,
German state and province, Switzers' Alpine country,
Each in turn have bound us like a magic spell.
Gazing on the mountains with the sunset glow
Resting o'er their summits crowned with white and snow,
What a sight imposing ! what a sea of grandeur !
With the roses sleeping in the vale below.

6 We have been in Asia, through the many countries
That to every Christian sacred still should be ;
We have stood in reverence where our blessed Saviour
Taught the crowds that gathered, taught them by the sea.
India's gentle breezes oft our cheeks have fanned ;
We have seen the sand-storms in old Afric's land ;
By the Nile we've wandered, where the rod of Moses
Brought the plagues of Egypt, at the Lord's command.

7 Time would fail to tell you more about our journey,
We must end our travels woven in a song ;
We shall try to picture scenes the most attractive,
Round the world of wonders while we passed along.]
Home again and happy, oh, how glad are we
Those we left behind us once again to see !
God protect our Union, God preserve our banner
Long to wave in triumph o'er the noble free.

SELF-DECEIVED.

PHILIP PHILLIPS.

"Wine is a mocker, strong drink is raging ; and whosoever is deceived thereby is not wise."—Proverbs 20, 1.

1. My heart is light and free ; My step is firm and strong ; I move a-mid the
2. I'm old-er than I was, I'm wis-er now to-day, Than when last year I
3. Car-ni-val joys I prize, To drive dull care a-way ; And oft-en quit life's

mul-ti-tude, The hap-piest of the throng, The wine is spark-ling red, Most beau-ti-ful to
danced and sang—The hap-piest of the gay ; My limbs are slight-ly weak, I trem-ble some, you
bus-y round To cheer the long dull day, My brain is o-ver-taxed With grave per-plex-i-

Largo.

see ; They say it glit-ters to de-ceive, But what is that to me ? O ! I am safe ! am
see, And brand-y need to calm my nerves, But what is that to me ? O ! I am saf-! am
ty, A glass of whis-key builds me up, But what is that to me ? O ! I am safe ! am

Chorus.

safe ! No dan-ger can I see ; The wine may ru-in you, per-haps, But can-not in-jure me.
safe ! No dan-ger can I see ; The brandy'if ru-in you, per-haps, But can-not in-jure me.
safe ! No dan-ger can I see ; The whiskey'll ru-in you, per-haps, But can-not in-jure me.

4 Ah, nothing harms me now,
All liquors tempt my thirst—
Old ale, and gin, and rum alike
Are good as wine at first ;
For drinking schools a man,
Sets him from bondage free ;
I'm not fastidious in my taste,
But what is that to me ?
O ! I am safe ! am safe ! no danger can I see ;
Strong drink will ruin you, perhaps, but
cannot injure me.

5 When I am asked to drink
I never answer, No ;
I cannot purchase it myself,
I daily poorer grow.
My living all is gone,
My clothes in rags you see ;
I take whatever I can beg,
But what is that to me ?
O ! I am safe ! am safe ! no danger can I
see ;
The rags might frighten you, perhaps, but
cannot frighten me.

6 I'm safe ! But am I safe ?
O ! what is that I see !
A yawning gulf before me lies,
A drunkard's grave for me ;
For me ! for me ! O, save !
Brave comrades, hear my call !
Stretch out a hand to rescue me ;
I tremble ! shiver ! fall !
Not one, alas, is safe ! but all who take the
glass,
And drink the brandy, rum, and gin, shall
feel its sting at last.

DESCRIPTIVE GUIDE

PHILLIPS' and Illustrated SONGS

TO PHILIP Illuminated TOURS

SYNOPSIS

UNITED STATES — Her Grandure and Greatness.
BRITISH COLUMBIA — Her Provinces and Cities.
AUSTRALIAN COLONIES — Their Resources and Wonders.
INDIA — Its Vastness, Idolatry and Beautiful Taj
HOLY LAND — Its Sights and Immortal History.
EGYPT — Her Dead Grandure, and the Nile.
ITALY — Its Burning Mountains and Cathedrals.
SWITZERLAND — Her Scenery and Mighty Alps.
GERMANY — Her Rhine and its Castles.
HOLLAND — The Land of the Pilgrim Fathers.
ENGLAND — Her Mightiness, and Metropolis of the World.
SCOTLAND — The Land of Scott and Burns.
IRELAND — With its bewitching Lakes of Killarney.

The whole forming a continuous journey of over 100,000 miles, occupying three nights.

EACH PROGRAMME ENTIRELY DIFFERENT.

Describing
HIS PERSONAL
TOURS
AROUND THE WORLD
AND THROUGHOUT
TWENTY COUNTRIES.

NEW YORK.
PHILLIPS PUBLISHING COMPANY.

Philip Phillips

Was born in western New York. His genius as a singer was discovered at an early age, and he is now acknowledged to be the pioneer of sacred and descriptive solo singing.

This distinguished position he has won and kept, being graciously welcomed wherever he goes, charming his auditors by his fine voice, amiability and modesty.

A few facts are worthy of mention concerning this, the only man who has belted the world with his SERVICES OF SONG.

He has given nearly 4,000 entertainments in aid of benevolent objects, paying his own expenses, and leaving a profit to different charities, of over $112,000. This large sum of cash has been distributed into every State in America, and also twenty other countries.

He has given his entertainments in each of the capitals, and chief cities and towns in every State of the Union. In Great Britain and Ireland he has visited every town of importance, from

Cowes in the Isle of Wight,
Douglas in the Isle of Man, to
Wick near Johnny Groat's land.

In one engagement of a hundred nights in Great Britain, there were 112,500 tickets sold leaving a net profit (after paying Mr. Phillips) of $1,445 for the purpose of establishing Sunday-Schools on the Continent of Europe.

By this means he has been of service to needy charities, helped himself along, and above all, left a refining influence wherever he has gone.

A few years ago, Mr. Phillips, accompanied by his family, left his home in New York for San Francisco. From thence he visited the Sandwich Islands, New Zealand, the Colonies of Australia, Tasmania, Ceylon, India, Egypt, Palestine, the Continent of Europe, England, and then back to America. They were three years on this tour of the world, and five hundred and seventy-four Services were conducted during that time.

In India four months were consumed in visiting the points of interest between Madras, Calcutta, North India and Bombay. The English-speaking population is so numerous in the Empire, that large audiences greeted him wherever he went.

In Australia the "Singing Pilgrim" was most heartily received, and for one hundred and forty-one nights lifted his voice in song, to the evident delight of all who heard.

In Cairo and Alexandria his songs were listened to with interest by good-sized gatherings, and especially did they cheer the hard-working missionaries on their way—who labor so incessantly for God's glory in those far-off fields.

Mr. Phillips regards his visit to Palestine as one of the most delightful memories of his world-wide peregrinations. There, in the old "City of David," was he privileged to sing the "Grand Old Story," and near the supposed manger where Christ was born, did he break forth with his song—

"I will sing of Jesus,
With his blood he bought me;
And all along my pilgrim way
His loving hand has brought me."

Loth to leave the hallowed surroundings of Jerusalem, they journeyed to Naples, stopping awhile in Sicily, and thence over the Continent of Europe.

Upon his several visits to Europe he has sung in nearly all the great centres, including Naples, Florence, Rome, Milan, Vienna, Prague, Dresden, Leipzic, Berlin, Paris, Hamburg, Bremen, Copenhagen, Stockholm, Upsala, Orebro, Gottenburg, Brussels, Antwerp, Rotterdam, The Hague, &c., &c. Among his latest travels he has sung in every parish of Jamaica, West Indies, and has completed an engagement of fifty consecutive nights in the same building in Amsterdam, during the great Exposition. At the close of this engagement he was presented with a testimonial in the form of an album, beautifully ornamented with silver and gold, signed by five hundred persons, in appreciation of his services.

The question naturally arises when we think of the foregoing facts, how can people of foreign languages understand his songs, or does Mr. Phillips speak many languages? The answer is simple enough, for his songs are translated wherever he goes, to suit the tongue of his audience, and distributed so that they can follow every sentiment with nearly as much pleasure or benefit as though they spoke or understood the English. He is the author of several books of Sacred Song, aggregating a sale of over five million copies, many of which have been translated.

He has experienced the novelty of singing his songs in English, while the audience joined in the verses in four different languages.

He has journeyed without accident, more than 250,000 miles. As a guide to this great journey, and the many wonderful sights attending it, this little book is now issued, and it is hoped that the descriptions—though necessarily short—may be of interest, especially to those witnessing the exhibition of his TOURS ILLUMINATED AND SONGS ILLUSTRATED.

BOUND WITH DESCRIPTIVE SONGS AND GEM SOLOS.

IN the first half of this new book, Mr. Phillips describes his travels and experiences at length, embracing a period of over twenty-five years of travel throughout every State in the Union, British America, and over twenty different countries, including a tour around the world. The story of his journeys is told in the most graphic manner, replete with anecdotes and incidents, at the same time accurately describing the many great cities of the world, together with the most striking scenes witnessed during a journey aggregating over 250,000 miles. The reader commences the journey at the metropolis of the Western Hemisphere—New York City—making a circuitous route throughout every State in the Union and across the American Continent. After the rambles in California and Oregon, the reader is taken from the Golden Gate to the Sandwich Islands, introduced to the King in his palace, sighting the Southern Cross, crossing the Equator to New Zealand, thence to Australia's oldest metropolis—Sydney—the gold fields of Victoria, the fern trees of Tasmania, kangaroo hunting in the interior, throwing the boomerang by the natives, thence to the cinnamon groves and devil dances of Ceylon, the temples of India, and the gorgeous display witnessed on the occasion of the Prince of Wales' visit, the heathen metropolis Benares, and the beautiful Taj Mahal, at Agra, together with the Parsees and Baboos of Bombay. Through the Suez Canal, with its strange sights, Egypt and her dead grandeur, Palestine, with her ever sacred events, Italy, with her art galleries and burning mountains, the Continent of Europe, all about Naples, Vesuvius, Rome, Milan, Venice, Berlin, the Alps, Paris, Netherlands, Belgium, Sweden, England (especially London), Scotland, with its highland beauties and noble history, Ireland with its bewitching Lakes of Killarney, across the Atlantic, to New York City; making a continuous journey West, until home again.

The work, in its completeness, forms a graphic Encyclopedia to the natural features, climate, various productions, manners and customs of the people in the different countries visited, ancient ruins, historical places, strange adventures, methods of living and traveling; all being portrayed to the reader scarcely less vivid than that of actual observation. The cities and places described are not from fancy, but from the pen of the author, who was an eye witness of them, in his tour around and throughout the world.

IT IS A WHOLE LIBRARY IN ITSELF; A PICTORIAL GAZETTEER OF THE WORLD; INTENSELY ENTERTAINING; A BOOK OF TRAVELS; A BOOK OF SONGS; AND ONE WHICH SHOULD BE IN EVERY HOUSEHOLD.

The second half of the book is entitled

Descriptive Songs and Gem Solos

In this department are found the Gem Solos, together with many choice selections, as sung by Mr. Phillips in his peregrinations around and throughout the world at over three thousand successful entertainments, which is a test and proof of their peerless merit. These songs are beautifully arranged with piano and organ accompaniment, and are now for the first time offered for sale in one book.

Many of these selections have been translated into different languages and sung in the largest and most important assemblages on earth, in presence of the magnates of nations, in Jerusalem, the city of the Great King, throughout the Australian colonies, under the Banyan trees of Ceylon and India, in the great capitals and cities of Europe, Crystal Palace, London, and from the isles of the sea to the four corners of the globe.

The book is bound with "Round the World," and the music alone is worth many times the price asked for the entire book. As early as in 1864, Mr. Phillips issued his

"Musical Leaves."—These songs were sung around the camp fires of our late civil war, and throughout the sabbath schools of our entire land. They had a total sale of over 700,000 copies. He next brought out that original and ingenious book entitled

"The Singing Pilgrim" and also "Song Life."—A most beautiful blending of the Bible and Bunyan in Christian song. These books have had a sale of more than 800,000 copies. In 1872 came forth

"Hallowed Songs,"—a book of Gems from many authors. This book was used by Moody and Sankey the first two years of their greatest success at home and abroad, and it reached the sale of nearly half a million copies, while his

"Song Sermons" and "Song Service" have had an aggregate sale of more than 900,000 copies. During the five different times he has visited Great Britain for the purpose of conducting his services of song, the London Sunday School Union have published his books, including "American Sacred Songster," "Song Life," "Musical Leaflets," etc., and they have sold in that country, between one and two millions of his publications. Mr. Phillips is admitted to be the pioneer singer of sacred song, at religious assemblies, and no man has been more original in his publications and methods, or more instrumental in leading others into the sweet service of Christian song. He has had a wider experience, and is therefore more capable of making a popular book of song gems than any other man, and he now offers the results of his efforts in this, the crowning book of his eventful SONG LIFE.

Agents will find this one of the most salable books, for old and young will buy it if properly presented. Should there be no canvassing agent in your vicinity, send at once for terms and prices to

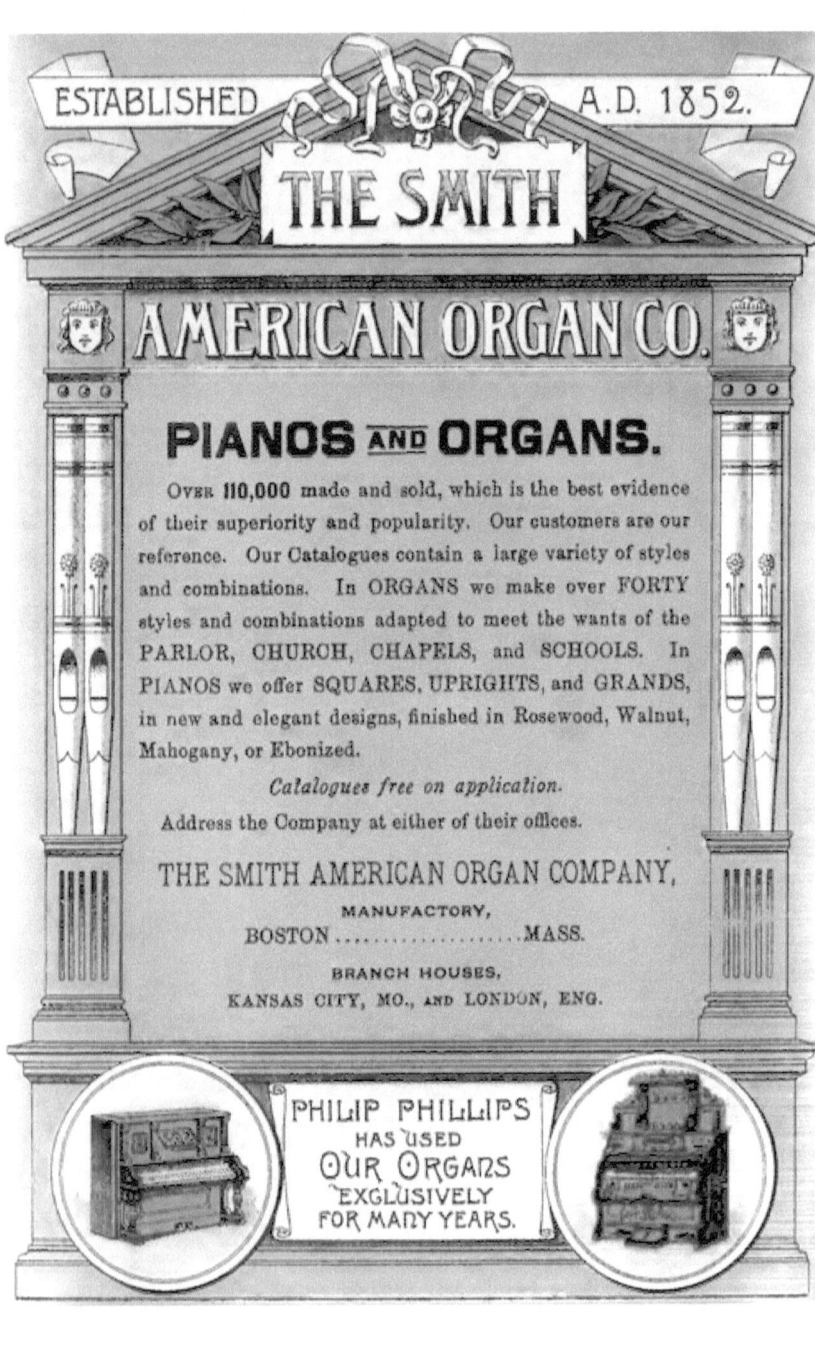